LONG DISTANCE

Books by Penelope Mortimer

LONG
DISTANCE

BY
Penelope Mortimer, 1918–

DOUBLEDAY & COMPANY, INC.
Garden City, New York 1974

This novel appeared originally in *The New Yorker* in somewhat different form.

Library of Congress Cataloging in Publication Data

Mortimer, Penelope, 1918–
   Long distance.
    I. Title.
PZ4.M887Lo   [PR6063.0815]   832'.9'14
ISBN 0-385-02771-0
Library of Congress Catalog Card Number 74–2721

For my mother, *Caroline Fletcher*.
And for all the characters, who are fictitious.

Those who cannot remember the past
are condemned to repeat it.
George Santayana

PART ONE

1

Mrs. April opens the door (a side door, one can always recognise them) in the same moment that she says, "I am Mrs. April." We smile, ask each other how we are doing, how we are. We go into a dark passage, out of the glare of the sun, and she leads me through what seem (I look eagerly through open doorways) to be kitchen premises, Mrs. April offering, I think, a rather tepid welcome. At least she doesn't ask me if I had a good journey, which is just as well, the mere word is enough to set me off again. It's all I can do, concentrating on Mrs. April's small back, not to go roaming off into the pantries and sculleries, the ironing rooms and lamp rooms and rooms for polishing boots, all with their own particularly powerful smell. You can get drunk inhaling steaming linen, paraffin and boot polish: they should be more careful.

We come out of these dingy tributaries into a large and splendid hall. I can't take it all in, the oak and marble, the brass and the bust. What I do notice is the silence, as Mrs. April briefly waits for me to be impressed. I notice the silence (of course, at least I've solved that) because of an indoor fountain which, presumably turned off, drips into a shallow pool.

"That is the dining room," Mrs. April says, indicating a closed door.

I nod.

"And that is the door to the terrace. We keep it locked from the inside."

I nod again. It would be more curious if it were locked from the outside.

Mrs. April starts up the stairs with the ease of a guide who no longer notices the stairs. I climb behind her, face raised and turning from one object to another, the great stained-glass window, the portraits, the lamps, many of which are switched on, even though there is plenty of daylight. We come to a spacious landing, a plateau, furnished with sofas. The walls are lined with books in dark covers, and again the lamps have been left on, though their light is barely visible. Passages and stairs go off this landing in all directions, but Mrs. April goes to the nearest door, unlocks it, opens it, saying, "And this is your room."

As in an hotel, the room is dark and—as I rather apprehensively approach the doorway—airless. If they knew I was coming, they could at least have had it ready. I hang about in the doorway while Mrs. April battles with something in the darkness: this turns out to be a blind, for at last, with a snap and a whir, it ravels itself and I see the room, large, placid and scattered with furniture. I wander in, brutally leaving Mrs. April to fight with the other two blinds, to beat with clenched fist on the warped windows, to open them, to close the screens once more (I realise I am already bitten, there is a swelling on my cheekbone and another behind one knee), to turn at last with a little smile, understandably exhausted.

"Well," she says, "there you are."

"Thank you."

"I expect you'd like to rest before dinner."

"No!" But I quickly subdue my voice. "No, really I'm not tired. What a lovely view." I am looking down on an enormous lawn; in the distance, straight in my line of vision, is an ornate pond with a statue; a wall of dark trees surrounds the lawn on three sides; immediately below me is a broad, flagged terrace with steps leading down to the lawn. I have a confused idea (or memory) that this would be an excellent place for amateur dramatics, *Dido and Aeneas* perhaps, I can hear the patter of applause in the twilight, see chair-legs (the chairs brought out from the house) sinking into the soft turf.

"Your bathroom is just across the passage," Mrs. April says. She is moving towards the door. "There's a bell for dinner, you'll hear it quite clearly. Oh—" she stops, wondering how she could have forgotten, "do you have a watch?"

"No. No, I don't."

"That's unusual."

"Is it?"

"Well . . . most people have watches."

"Really?" I wish I could start a discussion about watches, but somehow they don't mean anything to me. "Why do you ask?"

"We have to confiscate them. Temporarily, of course. Watches, telephones, television, newspapers—radios, of course . . ." Mrs. April seems dazed by the enormity of machinery beyond her comprehension. "All the pressures, you understand, of time and so forth . . . I mean, that is the whole point of being here."

I am wilfully stupid, in order to prolong the conversation, in order not to be left alone. "What? What is the whole point?"

"Well. First, to be relieved of the pressures. First, to be totally free."

"Totally?"

She smiles rather prettily. "Well, within limits, naturally."

"What are the limits?"

"You're expected to go to breakfast and dinner. To . . . help the staff as much as you can. Not to . . . upset the other guests." She seems a little uneasy, as though I've trapped her in some way. "You'll . . . remember in time," she says rapidly, almost beneath her breath.

5

"Remember?"

"This summer we have the pool, you'll like that." There's no doubt that Mrs. April is in difficulties, though surely she must be used to answering questions by now. "You must understand"—she laughs, this must be something she's often said before—"I'm really only what you might call a 'transit officer.' I don't take part at all in . . . running the place."

"What does that mean?"

"Well. I see people when they come—"

"And when they go?"

"Yes. And when they go."

"I have this problem at the moment. It tires me out."

"I expect so." She is guarded, but sympathetic.

"I keep running about all over the place. I can't seem to keep still."

Mrs. April sits on the arm of a chair, one hand neatly laid across the other. She has decided to stay for a few minutes. I am very relieved, though it means I must think of something more to say.

"For instance, just now I can't stop travelling."

"It's natural that just now you should have travelling on your mind."

"Yes, but I don't move, do I. Just think of the journeys I've made, the journeys you've probably made, Mrs. April—"

"Oh, no," she says. "I don't move about much."

"Well, I mean, sitting in a 'plane or a train or a car or even on the deck of a boat, for instance, or lying in the cabin of a boat, being moved forward, sometimes at really fantastic speed—but staying in the same place, do you see what I mean? Now an animal, an animal moves by itself, moves within itself. Wherever it goes, it . . . takes itself with it. Do you understand? It's obvious, of course. Bits of me keep getting stripped off and thrown out of the window, into the rushing wind."

"The rushing wind?" No wonder Mrs. April is puzzled.

"That's what it seems like. But of course it isn't. It's

just the . . . disturbance of the air, you see, made by the speed of the machine. It strips these pieces off you. Tears you up, you know."

Mrs. April nods. "What places," she asks, "do you have in mind?"

"Oh, good heavens . . . London, Santa Barbara, Mombasa, Sochi, Dublin, Bombay, Haslemere. I don't know where on earth I am. Piraeus or Evesham, Istanbul, Montreal . . ."

"All right," she says. "I see what you mean."

"Men used to hurtle round the moon, you know, or even further, strapped down like corpses. Perhaps they didn't even blink their eyes. When they got out and walked about—danced about, and somersaulted—they were attached to the machine all the time by a sort of umbilical cord. Inside the machine, of course, they didn't go anywhere. I find that terrible. Quite terrible."

"You've had a great many holidays," Mrs. April says, perhaps a little wistfully. "So many places."

"Well," I say, to excuse myself, "I was always running away."

"Really? From what?"

I know perfectly well, of course; and that it's not so much a question of from what as from whom (though perhaps they're the same thing, what and whom). I was, and still am, running away from the person to whom (in a sealed envelope, a bulky carton, a gift-wrapped package?) I had addressed my life. The name on the address is simply "you," partly because I still can't bear to name you specifically, and partly because I am beginning to suspect that you are not an individual at all but a composite of many individuals; that you do not live in one easily identifiable place, but in very many places at the same time; that your characteristics, unlike your thumbprint, are not unique to you but are those of an ethic, a way of oblivion, what Mann calls "an unconscious type," which I must either escape from or pledge myself to destroy. The pronoun "you" can be singular or plural. To answer Mrs. April's question truthfully, I should have to say that all these madcap excursions or escapades (which inevitably landed me, with ever-increasing speed and efficiency, in your bed) were attempts to free myself from you, to fly, drive, sail, ski, skate, travel across the boundaries of your horizon and find refuge in some totally different (and imaginary) climate.

I will not, however, answer Mrs. April truthfully. She has said herself that she is only a transit officer, and in any case I have sworn to myself not to speak of you to anyone. I shrug my shoulders, therefore, and say, "I don't know what from. It's the travelling itself that concerns me. The things lost, left behind, scattered about the place. The fact of being transported, you see, rather than actually moving. I can't understand it."

"You don't have to . . ."

I'm sure she's not going to say anything important. "But it could just as well be something else. Kitchens, for instance. I had to be very careful downstairs. The whole idea of kitchens, their variety, their complexity, can wear me out. Water. Books. Tablecloths. Seaweed. I can't stop myself speculating." I rap my forehead, to indicate the place. "Up here."

"You don't have to worry. He hasn't been here, he won't come here. Not, that is, unless you invite him."

"Invite? How would I do that?"

Mrs. April gets up. She is a busy woman, she has spent too much time with me, now I must fend for myself. "We shall see. In the meanwhile, as I told you, all arrivals and departures go through my hands, and I can assure you that you're perfectly safe as far as that's concerned. Do try to rest, now, until dinner."

"Trying to rest," I say feebly, with a feeble smile, "is a contradiction in terms."

"I probably shan't see you for a while. I hope you enjoy the pool."

"Thank you," I say. "I'm sure I shall."

"Don't forget the bell for dinner."

"I shan't. I'm very hungry."

"Good. Well, then. Take care of yourself."

The door closes. I am alone. God knows how long it is until dinner. Am I frightened? Yes. No one can possibly indulge in this experiment without fear. God knows (I am becoming slipshod) where it will lead me. I decide that rather than become a victim of myself, with its attendant dangers of having to travel vast distances by thought, I will, in as detached a manner as possible, examine my living quarters.

* * *

This is my room, where I shall live for an unspecified time, which you, if Mrs. April is to be believed, will never see: there are no less than four dressing tables, though only three have mirrors. The room measures twenty-seven of my feet by twenty-two; as I measure it (to be exact) I topple from side to side like a tightrope walker maintaining balance, I might be carrying a parasol or a long pole. There are three doors, the one leading to the outside paned with stained glass; the other two also paned with glass, latticed—one leads into a cupboard the size of a child's bedroom, the other is firmly locked and even by pressing my face against the glass I can see nothing but darkness. However, examining this more closely, I'm relieved to find that a piece of black cloth has been fixed behind the glass. It isn't darkness. The cloth has even sagged at the top and through the gap (by standing on a chair) I can see a perfectly ordinary patch of sky. Why not another room, though? I must be in the middle of the mansion, not the end. I must look up at my windows from the terrace and try to find out why, in an inside room, a side wall faces the open air.

In the window bay there is a desk clothed in thick brown paper, two hideous bronze lights springing from one stem, a sprig of some dead flower stuck into the mouth of a reproduction Cretan wine jar. Next to it (and I have already turned this towards the window) an upholstered rocking chair. My nun's bed, white and narrow, presses against the wall. Another bed, which will be unused, is across the room; they have attempted to heap it with two faded velvet cushions and a cardboard bolster, but it will positively not be heaped, it is too obviously spartan. A white-painted table which will be useful for books, and for the fruit I hope to save from meal-times. Two more tables from some auction lot; two adjustable armchairs with wooden frames, which I know I will never adjust; a vast wastepaper bin and a curious wicker stand for aspidistras or pampas grass, the wicker is black with age, at one time it may have been gilded.

Now I discover another door, a door that has no glass, a door that will not even budge enough to creak. It is hidden behind a tattered silk screen on which I can dimly see some sort of Chinese motif. God, I am suspicious of this door. I go outside into the passage—no sign of it. Where does it lead, then? Why do they try to hide it? Did they think I would never look behind the screen? Certainly I daren't touch it, in case it crumbles away. But I can see round it. Four doors in my room, and only one way out. It's not normal. I hope I never find out why they are there, I hope they are never opened.

The ornate light brackets will fall from the wall before long; they look as though they have been doctored by a succession of amateurs. The table lights are made from samovars, I think. They have chains for switches, and at least the chains look new. There are two brown engravings on the walls; one, of some pastoral scene, hangs crooked. I make this inventory, yet when I go over and sit in the rocking chair for a few moments, I can't picture it. This room is "now"; if only it were "then" I would know it better.

I decide, in order to keep moving, to go and look at my bathroom. This is very dangerous, and gives me a severe attack of speculation. My bathroom is a dining room (or study, possibly) panelled in oak, with innumerable cupboards and doors and a marble fireplace. The

shower, cramped in the corner, and the lavatory are
incidental. As it contains no bath, it can hardly be called
a bathroom; yet "washroom" would be inadequate for such
a dignified place. I know I shall never be able to clean
myself in it. The Romans, the Greeks, the Etruscans, the
most ancient civilisations (but oh, I am so tired) made
use of tiles when washing down their bodies. The sluicing
of water on tiles is immediately cleansing. This room comes
from the dark ages (but haven't I travelled far enough,
why don't I try to rest?) when bodies were stifled in
serge, dreadful diseases were kept hidden, there was a
tax on windows, the air was unchanged from winter to
winter (do the trees turn here, or are they evergreen?). It's
no use protesting, I am off and away. Bathrooms, then,
were made by the enlightened from bedrooms, living
rooms, or cupboards. My grandmother's is carpeted in that
most dreadful of synthetics, linoleum. My mother makes
me stand in very hot water and douses me with cold,
which she has heard is good for the circulation. My mother
believes my circulation is poor, that I am anaemic and
prone to tuberculosis; she has remedies for all these conditions and gives me sugar lumps soaked in eucalyptus
to cure my catarrh. In the so-called bathroom here there
isn't even linoleum, just bare boards on which to blot
one's feet.

I try to leave the bathroom, but it's no good, I'm
trapped. Of course the best bathrooms nowadays are once
again reception rooms, furnished with antiques and greenhouse plants; nevertheless, they have tiles, even though
they are art nouveau, or nineteenth-century Spanish tiles,
and their excellent plumbing is carefully disguised behind
William Morris wallpaper and swags of specially treated
velvet. In Bath itself (and other watering places, I suppose) the steam rises from ancient water, the smell is
metallic, the bathers are observed by sightless busts
with inclined heads, each curl and laurel leaf petrified
in stone. Mrs. April hopes I shall enjoy the pool, where
personally I hope that prisms of light will shake and

shatter deep in the blue water and I shall be able to immerse myself. Here, in this room, I shall dodge about in my shower like a child in a garden hose, the floorboards will get sodden, the soggy cracks in the wall open wider each day. I really don't know how I'm to keep clean. And you always said how clean I was, as though you thought it surprising, as though dirt, grime behind the ears, between the toes, inside the navel, was to be expected and found, in me, lacking.

As usual, I've managed to return to you, the escape is over. On the short way back to my room I notice the bookshelves on the landing and am almost off again, but manage to shut myself up in the nick of time. I am so hungry. Aren't they going to look after me, protect me at all? Total freedom within limits, Mrs. April said. I suppose this means that I, and the other people here, are free, within the confines of this freedom, to do anything we choose. Probably many of us, like myself, have temporarily lost the power of choice, but the alternatives—to walk or sit, to lie down or stand up, to go this way or that as far as the perimeter of the place—are there all the same. We have, I suppose, the freedom to do nothing at all, if such a thing were possible. I find it impossible. While waiting for the dinner bell, the sense of freedom oppresses me so much that I begin to sweat with fear. When I hear voices on the terrace, I jump up in the hope of being captured, or at least trapped in someone's notice.

A few people are sitting on the low wall of the terrace. None of them look up. I frantically search the tops of their heads, balding or curly, sleek or overgrown. I see their shoulders, their hands, their feet a long way off. Which one will be my friend? Which of these anonymous, quietly chattering people will share some of my appalling freedom with me? Perhaps they are waiting for me; or perhaps they will resent my intrusion. I can't make up my mind whether to go down and join them or not. Nobody has told me what to do. The indecision is so painful that, in order to resolve it, I sit down again in the rocking chair. If any of them happen to look up, they won't know I'm here. I have stolen a march on them, seeing them first.

The bell for dinner. I lean forward and peer over the sill. They all stand up and begin to walk indoors, out of my sight. What shall I do? (A notice on one of the dressing tables says that all valuables must be deposited in the safe, the management cannot be held responsible. My only treasured possessions are inside my head, or whatever part of my body takes care of such things. I am not going to lock my room.) I stand up—the chair rocks like an idiot's head for a few moments—and walk across the threadbare red carpet and open my door, the only one of my four doors that leads anywhere.

2

I wonder whether we are allotted particular places for meals. Apparently not, as there is a dignified scramble in the dining-room doorway and a gaunt man runs down the stairs past me, two and three stairs at a time, without giving me one look, let alone a second. This alarms me so much that I decide to pretend, for as long as I can, that I'm alone. I know this is an old trick of mine (like clenching my toes inside my shoes) and that it gives me an appearance of devastating and off-putting superiority, but I can't help it, I have to survive.

I don't, therefore, look at anyone as I wait in the queue for my food. I look at the mammoth and almost indiscernible paintings, the ornamental china, the furniture, the cutlery, a nonexistent scratch on my forearm. I step forward, unable to prevent myself from noticing the girl in front of me, who is made of instant porridge (gruel would perhaps be more correct. She is lumpless, without grain of any kind. Her skin, like the skin of instant porridge, is cellophane-thin, with little but water beneath). The girl, I note from under my indifferently lowered eyelids, seems to be in a state of deep depression. She is concave, dressed in a brown turtle-neck sweater (in spite of the weather) and jeans. Her abundant hair is colourless, her hands hang at her sides, she shuffles forward as though not caring at all what she will receive in the end, if you gave her a lottery ticket or a glimpse of Lenin it would be all the same.

A man's voice says, "Zotkind," or something of the sort. I turn, startled, thinking it must be a profanity, or a criticism of my apparent disdain. The small, burly man smiles in his beard. "Gotzink," he says holding out his hand, "Basil."

"How do you do?" I shake his hand.

"Hi."

"Hi," I reply. As though we were two Indians meeting on a mountain pass.

"You got here all right, then?"

"Yes. Yes, I did."

"Quite comfortable? Settling in okay?"

"Yes. Thank you."

As we inch forward, Gizdonk continues to chatter, exuberant. His beard, bristling and curling and spiked with grey, must, I imagine, complement his pubic hair. He has been swimming, he tells me, and indeed his head, though not his beard, is still wet. Dressed in shapeless trousers which completely disguise him from the waist down (odd how one has come to appreciate that coxcomb bulge, as alluring to women as a sweatered breast is said to be to a man) and a yellow knitted shirt, he dances forward as though in training. Indeed I know already, before I know him at all, that he enjoys ball games and all forms of athletics. His small eyes glint behind gold-framed spectacles. His mouth, two perfect lips obscured by all that harsh hair, coyly refutes all the brazen masculinity. He gestures with small, impeccable hands, the fingernails longer than my own. He seems to be on tremendously amiable terms with everybody. I feel I am being invited into the fold.

Nevertheless, I do not want to eat my dinner with Gidzink or the porridgy girl, the one obviously demanding too much of me, the other totally indifferent. The girl, receiving her plate of food (chicken, of course, a meat which hasn't been edible since I was a child, a meat for those who inanely believe that a chicken doesn't have as much red blood, relatively speaking, as a cow, a mass-produced meat with as much flavour and nourishment as wadding—all this I will tell Zigdonk later, and he will disagree with me passionately), the girl sits at the nearest pseudo-Jacobean chair, filling up the centre table. I must broach an empty table entirely, daring Godzonk to follow me. I sit (I hope) as though about to preside at family dinner. Nozdik inevitably follows me. I cannot say this place is reserved. He sits. I busy myself with my chicken, for I am hungry. The table fills up with other people, all of whom seem to have anxiety or euphoria moving behind their guarded eyes.

At first the conversation is general, hardly including me. A red-haired man called Paul, who titters, has spent a pleasant afternoon on the croquet lawn in the company, it seems, of some relative. I am sure we are not allowed visitors (in spite of Mrs. April's hint that I might invite someone) and don't understand it. A tiny, rather hectic young woman (Rowena?) teases Zidgonk about his swimming; I feel she is teasing him about something else. A serious, very neat man, Revlon, says he has heard that they are misusing the Repair Fund, they are going to build tennis courts instead of seeing to the sewer. Gizdink is very interested in this news. He notes that it is getting dark early this evening, and leans across me to switch on the table lamp, which makes a pool of light at which our faces can lap gratefully. He then questions Revlon, agreeing that the misuse of the Repair Fund is a scandal and suggesting ways in which, as guests of the place, we can protest. As he talks, quietly and forcefully, I think I begin to recognise him.

I hear his voice asking me a question. "Not working?" he asks, pretending to chide me as I wander (while eating my chicken?) through a fairyland of electric lights, a forest of floor lamps so bizarre that I can only wonder, of standard and desk lamps, of lamps angle-poised for reading or petit-point, of strip lights and lanterns. And above, as that "Not working?" whispers down the brilliant corridors, a lunatic roof of chandeliers and dazzling balloons, of orange hexagons and bowls of light. "No" I say, "I'm trying to buy a lamp, but how expensive they are." He realises, then, that I am trying to economise. Perhaps he thought I was rich. I am so bold in the brilliant setting. "Ring me," I say, giving him my number (in those days, I think, telephone exchanges had beautiful names, Primrose if not Eglantine, Juniper and Mulberry, Hope and Grief perhaps, Modesty and Love). In the afternoon, when I am lying on my bed in a darkened room, he will telephone, and I will ask him over for a drink.

In the meanwhile, his serious conversation over, he tells me that he is learning to swim. It is a marvellous achievement. He is horizontal, thrashing the water with powerful arms, no longer fearing to drown. He has grown heavier, more rabbinical. I wonder whether he has retained his zest for love and why he doesn't make the slightest sign of recognition. I can't have changed that much. I will caress him with luxurious creams, economising on other things, but he talks about swimming. Odd that his eyes aren't still for a moment. I prefer them ponderous with lust. Keep your eyes still, Zidgonk or whoever you are, float and be still. Now sleeps the crimson petal, sings my father, mellow-voiced, now the white, now sleeps the goldfish in the porphyry font, so fold thyself, my dearest one, and slip into my bosom and be lost in me. "Come and watch me," he says, cramming himself with chicken, "I like to be watched, it gives me confidence."

There is no way of finding out who set that poem to music. Dinzok certainly won't know. Trivial little bits of information like that, and they won't tell you. I begin to be irritated, a sure sign that I'm out of my depth.

"This time thing," I say, "seems affected to me. I mean, it's ridiculous to try and make us do without time."

"Maybe there's an alternative?"

"Maybe with acid or prayer or meditation. Maybe if we were all stoned out of our minds. You can't do much with chicken and ice water."

This is where we have our argument about chicken. Neither of us is persuaded. Gozdik has a white band on his wrist, where he must have quite recently worn a watch. It is, I know, a mediocre watch with a black dial, not only telling him the time but the date as well. Not, however, the year. It could be 2875 (A.D.) and my mother coming up to her thousandth birthday. Even outside, Gidzonk's watch couldn't tell him that, but would plod on accumulating minutes, hours and numbered days as though the present—that precise moment after the third stroke—were all that mattered.

"Why do they have all those books about?" I ask. "If we're supposed to be forgetting time."

"Perhaps some books are timeless," he says unctuously.

"Huh," I say, full of trepidation and contempt.

"'She is older than the rocks upon which she sits, like the vampire she has been dead many times, and has learned the secrets of the grave, and keeps their fallen day about her'?"

"Well?" Tennyson and Pater are improbable companions at this (in spite of the lamp) daylight dinner. "Do you think Charles Kingsley liked swimming?"

"Maybe. I think he equated it with moral hygiene."

I laugh. I am beginning to like Gonzink, in spite of his passion for chicken. He is now eating pink ice cream, shovelling it into his beard like a ten-year-old.

"I suppose you think it's romantic, Byronic, to be a strong swimmer."

"In point of fact," he says, delicately wiping ice cream off his whiskers, "I'm more like Shelley."

"Who drowned."

"Exactly."

What we're doing with all these nineteenth-century poets I have no idea. Zinkgot turns to talk to Rowena. Someone at the next table (where the depressed girl stares at the plate she has made so clean that it is ready for the dishwasher) says loudly, "Oh, he brought his brief case of course," and everybody except the girl laughs. And yet I know that if I ask who brought the brief case and when and where, they will look at me as though I were simple. I am excluded, my only adventure a meeting in the electrical department with Donzik, who doesn't appear to remember. I look forward to going back to my room, where I can sulk in private.

That, however, is not his plan. We will walk round the lake, he says. I don't want to do this, to be devoured by insects so that I shall scratch all night like a cat, long, vicious strokes making white tracks on my skin. More than this, I think I know where any kind of deepening intimacy will lead: it will end in tears, in recrimination and disgust. I will be trying to make telephone calls from a wayside call box without the appropriate money. I will take to humiliation like a duck to water. Ginkzok, after a restoring holiday, will marry and have two children. He will marry a girl with prominent hip-bones, a deeply indented waist between hip and rib as she lies on her side, cheek on hand, watching him dress for work. I can avoid all that by taking a short cut to my present indifference; though already I am dismayed to find the indifference tinged with affection.

No, I don't want to walk round the lake. I don't want to go through that again. And yet it seems, with all this freedom, that I have no free will, for I hear myself saying, "Yes, I would like to walk round the lake. How big is it?" and he replies that it is not big at all, more of a pond really. He tells me that we must stack our plates and take them to the kitchen, there are very few servants (and those there are, from my glimpse of them, look and behave more like matrons, nurses, nannies, people in authority). Then we leave, followed by many curious glances. Nizdok and I are leaving together: that is the news.

He bounces along. I hurry to keep up with him. We go down a driveway, he points out the pool through a clump of pine trees.

"And the office," he says, throwing an arm in the opposite direction, "is over there. Would you like to see it?"

"Why? Is there anything special about it?"

"No. I just wondered if you'd like to see it."

"I suppose it has notice boards and filing cabinets and in trays and out trays just like other offices, doesn't it?"

"I expect so. You know in the winter, if you stand still, your feet freeze to the ground."

"You've been here in the winter, then?"

He hesitates, looks at me oddly, then asks me if I swim. He is obviously obsessed with swimming.

"A little."

"How much? Two lengths? Four lengths? Twenty?"

"I've never counted."

He shakes a finger at me. "I bet you do twenty."

"Maybe six."

"Six, huh? Interesting."

Now I am almost running to keep up with him.

"When do they empty the pool?"

"The meadows," he says, with a nonchalant wave of his hand towards an open space beyond the trees.

We can make love in the meadow, not in a corner or on the edge of it but bang in the middle, without shelter. We won't realise until afterwards that a man has been watching us from behind the trees; when we do, we will be offended that there is no applause, the slow clapping of a pair of hands in the stillness would be impressive. I can't make out whether Zondik knows this, has forgotten it, or merely takes it for granted. The track winds through pine trees, the soft ground treacherous with needles. There are a few huts in the woods, possibly (I shudder) for solitary confinement, the food passed through a small trap door, cat door (which lets in a cold wind, whistling along the hallway. When the cats, Troilus and Pushkin, have been sent away to grow lean and ferocious in the country, the cat door is sealed up with insulating tape; but still it lets in the wind). But I will only ask him one more question.

"You told me your name, but I didn't hear. What is your name?"

"Basil." He is named for a herb, I know that.

"But your second name?"

"Gondzik. G-o-n-d-z-i-k."

"Really? Gondzik?" It is a relief, really. I thought he was going to say Greenstreet, and tell me that it had originally been Grunheim but his father had it changed on account of the war. The air is lighter after a humid day. It even becomes slightly chilled as we reach the lake.

"Cold?" he asks, though I don't know why, there is nothing he could do about it.

"No, it's not cold."

He stands looking along the shore of the lake, perhaps wondering which way to go. Like a dog he stiffens, becomes intent. I see nothing yet but the lake, the pines, the muddy little waves lapping on mud. He shivers shortly, slaps his arms round himself, his face changes. As cautiously as a mother approaching a child on a rooftop I take one step towards him on the soft turf; wait; ask almost inaudibly, "What is it?" He turns and smiles, teeth as pretty as the mouth in all that hair. He puts his arm round my shoulders and begins to walk towards his vision, or whatever it was.

My mother, in devoted evenings, made a suit for Hiawatha, from the red deer's hide Nokomis made a cloak for Hiawatha. Now, caught completely off my guard, it is I who am diverted and enchanted. Sunlight through the pine trees dapples her dress as I track her down upon one knee uprising, pull the bow and aim the arrow winging to fall just short of her lap by this shore of Gitche Gumee. The moon is a paring in the pale sky, dangling above the pine trees. Once a warrior, very angry, seized his grandmother and threw her up into the sky at midnight, what shocking behaviour for a warrior. We are in a vast stadium, my mother and I, my eyes stretch with wonder, down the aisles and through the stadium, down the river o'er the prairies came the warriors of the nations, came the Delawares and Mohawks, came the Choctaws and Camanchos, came the Shoshonies and Blackfeet, came the Pawnees and the Omawhas, came the Mandans and Dacotahs, came the Hurons and Ojibways. I block my ears at the black-robe chief and his soppy talk and wait full of exultation, pretending for the moment I'm in church and needn't listen.

On the shore stands Hiawatha, turns and waves his hand at parting, on the clear and luminous water, attached to an elaborate system of pulleys, launched his birch canoe for sailing, from the pebbles of the margin shoved it forth into the water, whispered to it, "Westward! Westward!" and with speed it darted forward away, away for ever, into the wings of the enormous stadium, sailed into the fiery sunset, sailed into the purple vapors, sailed into the dusk of evening. "Did you enjoy it?" my mother asked, unsure. Dumbfounded, streaming, I nod my head again and again, knowing I should say thank you.

It is useless, I know, to ask Gondzik who wrote the music, or what "Onaway" means for that matter. My father sings, anyhow: Onaway! Awake, beloved! It's a clarion call, followed by rushing footsteps: thou, the wild flower of the forest, thou, the wild bird of the prairie, thou (emphatic, singling me out) with eyes soft and fawn-like! Confidential: if thou only lookest on me, I am happy, I am happy, as the lilies of the prairie, when they feel . . . the dew upon them. Urgent, so urgent: does not all the blood within me leap to meet thee, leap to meet thee, as the springs to meet the sunshine in the Moon when nights are brightest—Onaway! There is a sad bit now, he is wretched, but soon he goes rollicking on, smiles the earth and smile the waters, smile the cloudless skies above us . . . oh awake, awake, beloved! Onaway! Awake, beloved! How he sings with his great chest.

"He should have been a concert singer. They all said so."

"But he was happy in the Church?"

"In the Church? Oh, no. He wasn't at all happy. He had to take pills to calm his libido."

"That's how he put it?"

"That's what he told me."

Realising that I have used a past tense, I suddenly feel very lonely, outcast rather than foreign.

"Who is the sad girl in front of me in the queue?"

"Elizabeth. She's not so much sad as simple. I stayed with her one night."

"Here?" I am astounded, jealous.

"She begged me."

How, I wonder, do you beg. She squats on the floor between his mammoth legs, she holds up her paws, simple head on one side, begging for the bone hidden within those folds of Terrylene. When he gives it to her, she whimpers with delight, buries it in a secret place. But you are a modest man, Gondzik, I think; modest and gentle; cataclysmic, apocalyptic only in love; you don't favour beggars pawing at your breeches.

"I don't understand."

"Oh, well." He shrugs it off, no longer patient. "She clung to me. Like a little girl."

This is certain to disgust me. He has hit it right on the nose, scored a bull's-eye. What has happened to you, Gondzik? Where has your bony young wife gone, the children you carry on your shoulders? You have left them outside, no doubt, but even so . . . Also I notice that he has been referring to some nonexistent past, a night we have left behind.

The insects attack me. They nuzzle up under my long dress, seeking out the fleshier parts of my body, nipping and stinging. I suggest haughtily that we go back, and he agrees. We are unco-ordinated, but I have no idea whether the part I know is over or whether it is yet to come; whether perhaps it is happening now, and I have forgotten.

That is all that happens on our walk. Inside the house a huge Brandenburg is playing, nobody is there to listen. Music, of course, is timeless. Gondzik comes with me up the stately stairs, the indoor fountain drips monotonously, the pre-Raphaelites squint down their long noses. Outside my room he kisses me good night. His lips and teeth have disappeared, he gnaws at me with open jaws, but not for more than a few seconds. I know they are seconds because

I am counting one two three four at the rate of a slow heartbeat.

I am in my room, the door closed. It is getting dark. Like a Christian in a pagan country I fold my hands and say, "The day is over"; but not aloud in case the rickety light fittings are bugged, which now seems not unlikely.

3

In a dream in the night I see myself walking away from you down an endless grass path, the borders of which meet only in infinity. I walk backwards as easily as though I had eyes in the back of my head; I will be facing you long after you are out of sight. It is very important to make sure that I am in myself as I walk, float, drift backwards along the path. Between the petunias, the pergolas, the small box hedges. It is vitally important that no part of me remains in you, static on your stone bench spattered with bird lime; that I do not look out through your eyes, for if I did I would lose sight of myself, my poor self would be abandoned, hollow, lighter than air, to step backwards for . . . to step interminably.

Waking, I review the situation. Not too bad, but not very satisfactory either. I don't know how long I have been here, possibly weeks by now, and certain things trouble me. My relationship with Gondzik remains, on the surface, exactly as it was left after our walk round the lake. He is proprietary towards me, and always kisses me good night; sometimes when we are lying by the pool he strokes my bottom, thinking of something else, as though it were a cat. He doesn't wish to get further involved with me, believing, for some reason, that I have suffered too much and would interfere with his mirth. Gondzik's mirth expresses itself in loud shouts of laughter, and he is probably right. On the other hand, the loud shouts of laughter are frequently occasioned by idle remarks of mine, which are not all that funny. What he tells me of his sex life seems extraordinarily dour in that it is pornographic, and nobody with a sense of the ridiculous can appreciate pornography.

As Gondzik has, for the time being at any rate, taken me over, I get little chance to get to know anyone else. I could protest, but the security of having a relationship (however tenuous) so early on in my stay is too comforting. I have the impression that Gondzik's status is a little different from the others—something to do with his familiarity with the staff, perhaps, or the fact that I know that he often goes out after I have gone to bed. He is very concerned with the felonies of the administration, and probably meets with Revlon to decide what should be done. On the other hand, he may be feeding Elizabeth. From her increasingly haggard and dejected look, I would doubt it.

I wake early—it is barely light—and lie first on this side, then that, over on to my stomach, trying to investigate my uneasiness. Some people, I am almost sure, have rendezvous with outsiders; or they come upon the outsiders by chance, in the gardens or woods; or the outsiders are put in their path by some meddling authority. If this is so, it's an infringement of freedom. Yesterday I asked Paul, the red-haired man with the titter, whom he had spent the afternoon with on the croquet lawn. He simply looked at me, puzzled, and walked away. And yet I distinctly heard him say . . . and yet I don't know, perhaps I was mistaken. When alone, I keep strictly to the pool path. By keeping to this path, my destination obvious from my towel and sun-oil and general paraphernalia, I intend to resist any such encounter. I intend to do what I was told (I think?) and wait, if necessary for life, for time to do its work. Once I can get the hang of it, I may even learn to control my dreams. I suppose some sort of immortality isn't entirely out of the question.

In spite of my association with Gondzik, I don't show any interest in the stories of corruption, the lies and bribery and other political gossip. I don't join in the speculation. I do object, though, to the behaviour of some of the guests. However critical they are of the administration, they are not above rifling through each other's personal possessions in the hope of gaining evidence, damning or otherwise. If rooms are left unlocked, like mine, they sneak in to examine passports for dates of birth (the gaunt man who appears to be in his mid-fifties is, they say, only thirty; the skittish blonde in the bikini is fifty-two); they flick through private diaries, they read the labels on medicine bottles, in case they can report anything illegal. All this seems perfectly justifiable to them, they even boast about it. I don't understand why the managers or directors, members of the administration, are supposed to be less fallible or prone to moral degeneracy than they are. Gondzik seems to think it isn't a matter of morality but principle. Much of the time, to be truthful, I haven't the faintest idea what Gondzik is talking about.

He can't answer a direct question, that's for sure. The question of the books, for example: "some books are timeless," how does that explain the inconsistency of having them here? With their bleak covers, often with gold lettering, they belong in some attic or second-hand store, indubitably past over and done with. To prove this, their subversive relation to time, the mere look of them transports me, more swiftly than any machine, to a first-floor loft in Petersfield, Hampshire. I am edging along the aisles, the floorboards creak, I am craning my neck to read the titles on the upper shelves: *The Letters of Franz Liszt*, *The Great Events by Famous Historians*, the collected volumes of *Punch* from 1845–87, *Poems* by William Vaughn Moody, *Happy Day or the Confessions of a Woman Minister*, *The Saga of the Norse Kings* in four volumes. A little Bertrand Russell, to bring us up to some long-forgotten date; Shaw

27

and Trotsky. While painfully reading these titles (in Peters-field) I am feeling love and anger and anxiety specifically related to time, I am troubled by old and irrelevant un-happiness. For these books to be here, where we are meant to be totally free, is a crying shame.

What is their purpose, I wonder. Some sort of test? I've been tempted, it's true, to open *The Married Life of the Frederic Carrolls* by Jesse Lynch Williams. In fact, I gave in, but only to find such phrases as "the next day," "the week before," "at that moment"; so I shut it again, feeling— as I suppose I was intended to—guilty. Nothing, I'm sure, is inadvertent in this place, everything is planned, every book catalogued over in the office. The office has the answer to all my questions—is that why Gondzik asked if I would like to see it, was he hinting at something? If one could see their files, their records . . . but that's not the way to do it. There may be a way, but not by breaking and entering at night. They certainly have a system of alarums, I can imagine the whole place pealing, searchlights sweeping the secret crannies of the woods.

I swing out of bed, frightened. Whatever time it is, I'm going to get up. The lawn is misty, the statue in the lily pond rises out of mist. I go to my bathroom and hurl my-self at the shower, fighting the hard stream of water with clenched eyes, letting it batter on my spine. As I'm drying myself, the bell rings for breakfast. I am always a little late.

Breakfast is more of an ordeal than dinner. No one feels any enthusiasm for the immoderate gift of time; we wish we could just have an hour, maybe forty minutes, we could be grateful for that. The blonde, who works nights, comes dressed for breakfast in chiffon. Paul wears a track suit and his smile. Rowena cowers in the corner of her chair. Revlon is immaculate, and most of the others put on clothes of some sort, but I resolutely wear a dressing gown. Gondzik is always early, the temperature of his energy already above normal. I avoid him at breakfast, if I can, being too full of fears of a private nature.

This morning Revlon, our illicit newsvendor, has a most surprising rumour: "It's Sunday," he says, looking straight ahead, not moving his lips. This means, if he's correct, that yesterday was Saturday and tomorrow will be Monday, we can calculate that seven lights and darknesses from now it will be Sunday again. With a twinge of excitement I pass on the news, in the same way, to Rowena; she, disguising it with a yawn, to the gaunt man; and so on, round the table. It's a good thing Gondzik isn't sitting with us, he wouldn't realise the significance of this fact (or rumour) and might blurt it out, causing distress and even punishment to someone.

My father prepares for Church, for matins; in his cassock with the black cummerbund (no popery purple for him) he strides about with the look of a busy man, barges through the swing door into the kitchen in search of coffee, digestive biscuits, any form of nourishment. He was up long before breakfast, administering the bread and wine. My mother and I cut the bread, holding sharp knives with both hands, chopping the inferior bread (my mother would never serve such stuff) into neat cubes: the Body. The Blood is kept in the vestry, which smells mouldy as my bathroom. The bell ropes, with coloured tapes like maypoles, hang down from the tower. When the bell-ringers come, taking off their jackets to get to work, the noise is so clamorous we can't hear ourselves speak and the babies cry. I am now hearing church bells as they should be heard, from a great distance, the skilful downward scale, the broken chords so melancholy they break my heart. My soul doth magnify the Lord, now lettest thou thy servant depart in peace, At matins we have the *Te Deum*, which in my head I write *Tedium*. My mother's stomach rumbles—how can she leave her endless chores for so long? I try to lift the heavy, dead-heavy hassock between my feet and am told off by one flick of my mother's hazel eye. O worship the King/all glorious above/O gratefully sing/His power and His love/Our shield and defender/the ancient of days/Pavilioned in splendour/and girded with praise. How I relish that pavilioned in splendour, rolling it round my tongue, sucking on it.

My father, with perfect enunciation saved for Sundays and the reading aloud of Browning, implores us from the high pulpit to believe in Life. I am, he calls sonorously, the Resurrection and the Life. This tormented man, who has only once played a childish game with me, who despises jokes and is unable to recognise irony, requires us to be Joyful, full of Joy. I can romp along with a God pavilioned in splendour, but all this is beyond me. What joy? The rooms are dense with his unhappiness, which no one can relieve. He will play the piano after church, some doleful dirge, and a few favoured neighbours will come for china tea in shallow cups, little biscuits with icing on the back, sometimes brandy snaps. I am so awkward on Sundays, getting in everybody's way. My mother is distracted (there's still the joint and vegetables to come, the suet pudding or rhubarb pie, we eat the huge bounty of my mother's cooking and grow fatter and fatter, my skin protests in acne, the afternoons are loaded with sleep) and my father overworked. Was this the greatest sermon of them all? Has it changed the world, will it be headlined in *The Times*, will great men write him letters of thanks, will girls wash his feet in their tears? The tea, the biscuits, the joint, the pudding, the sleep. That is all. My heart, broken by the bells, bleeds for my father. Here there is no such time as too late. Sunday is a terrible day. I wish it were Tuesday, a day of reasonable hope.

Gondzik with his interminable history of Sabbaths (now ostensibly discarded), won't appreciate the taste, smell and weight of this day. Neither will the simple Elizabeth, who hardly notices whether it is light or dark. Paul of the red hair and pink skin and silly smile is off giggling in a world of his own (found on the croquet lawn?). Revlon will spend the day as always, with his ear to the ground to detect some distant knocking, hammering or shovelling, that will give him a clue as to what they are up to over in the office. Although he knows it is Sunday (unless he mistook the signals) it doesn't seem to have occurred to him that offices close on Sunday, if he hears anything it will be the burrowing of moles or the tapping of earthworms. The silly blonde picks threads from her negligee, her work (of being sexually attractive) never done, men make as many demands on the seventh day as any other and she's only got one pair of hands. The geriatric thirty-year-old feeds himself with cereal, never speaking above a vague mumble, and then always of customs far more ancient than an Anglican Sunday; I don't know why he was allowed to bring his anthropology with him, unless he is one. They can't after all, separate people from what they are.

So I go to my room, heavy with breakfast and loneliness. They can give us all the time in the world but they can't stop the past increasing day by day, a lengthening shadow. Such subversive thoughts are more suitable for twilight, when the weight of food and the exquisite melancholy of Evensong come together to create a state near ecstasy, a kind of trembling on the brink of wisdom that is almost unbearable. Afterwards, we schoolgirls go and moon in the rose garden, languish lingeringly by the lily pond. We fall in love with each other, trail our hands in the brown water, write Sunday poetry full of sighs and sorrow. Never again is our theme at the age of fifteen or so: nevermore. It is true. Never again shall we be so near our *nunc dimittis*, nevermore feel so keenly the bliss of dying. We are doomed to Monday's racket, to men and children, uncomfortable journys, shopping lists, anxiety, the manipulation of dishwashers and washing machines and vacuum cleaners and cars; to lotions and vitamin-enriched creams, hair conditioners and deodorants, pots of this and that collecting in drawers and cupboards, hairgrips, Tampons to staunch the sea of blood (which Gondzik revels in, gleefully breaking ancient laws?). We are doomed to become wombs on legs, to make telephone calls without the appropriate money, to beg, plead, blackmail, weep, to make a terrible noise about living. How distressing, after the luminous melancholy of Sunday. I could become a nun, perhaps. Fold my hands just so. Glide on castors down cloisters, my eyes downcast. After all that din, the peace of Guinevere.

The most approximate element, in the meanwhile, is water. I will go and float in the pool, folding all my sweetness up. Collecting together insect repellent, oil, towel, finding my way confidently through the maze of passages, past closed doors, across unused lounges, escaping I think, from Sunday, I set out.

4

The way to the pool is very straightforward, but for the first time—perhaps because of my walk with Gondzik—I lose it and find myself in the vegetable garden, most bewildered. The vegetable garden is large, surrounded by a thick brick wall against which grow nectarines, peaches, plums and (in their season) apples. The ornamental iron gate is missing—fallen at last from its rusty hinges, or sold for scrap in some emergency—which is why I wander straight into the garden. If there had been a gate, I would not have opened it.

Screwing up my eyes against the sun, I look down the borders of Aaron's rod, poppies and old man's beard, towards the greenhouses. A man in shirt-sleeves is digging laboriously, his back to me, his right foot pushes the spade into the hard earth, then he loosens the earth and throws a spadeful aside, his distant back grim as a gravedigger. Assuming (not without reason) that he is a gardener, I loaf past the strawberry bed, approving the crimson berries lying in straw, enjoying the change of scene. But they have everything here, black and red currants, gooseberries bursting out of their skin, loganberries, raspberries. The asparagus thrives in its trench; row upon row of delicate carrot ferns marshalled in front of the taller potato leaves;

cabbage and cauliflower and broccoli, none of it gone to seed; sweet peas and rhubarb, green beans climbing up green string, abundant peas (I reach over the low, clipped hedge, wrench a pod from the stalk, split it with my thumbnail, eat each nestling pea deliberately, while longing to cram them all at once into my mouth). Broad beans too, regiments of freshly watered lettuce; marrow squash basking in the sun, a field of spinach. This man is a good gardener. I am no good at anything, deterred by my mother's skill with cuttings, clippings, annuals, biannuals, perennials, dividing, pruning and other mysteries. However, she doesn't grow vegetables, leaving that side of the thing—as she leaves repairs to anything but clothes, all forms of electrical work, coal heaving and log sawing—to her husband. And yet how sensible, how satisfactory to grow food. My mouth waters, appetite stirs.

I am now at the opposite end of the garden, walking slowly along beside the greenhouses (carrying this weight of aerosol sprays, towel and book) towards the gardener. I see, behind glass milky and old as a cataract eye, ripe tomatoes no larger than grapes, pot after pot of geraniums. The door of one of the greenhouses is open and I take a lungful of that particular humid air, hear the drip of water in a rusty tank. I'm tempted to go inside, drink a tomato after piercing its skin with my teeth. But the gardener, straightening, has his eye on me. I manage a timid smile, bumping the bag against my bare legs, feet dragging along the path.

I have never seen a man sweat so generously. Torrents of sweat pour down his face and neck into the collarless shirt, which he might just as well not be wearing. His grey flannel trousers are hitched high with braces; inside them he must be swimming. He is, to me, old: an old, burly man wiping the sweat out of his eyes with the back of his forearm, peering at me.

"Dinnertime, is it?"

I don't know what to say, just hang about, afraid of passing him.

"Well, then." He sticks the spade in the earth with a final gesture, lumbers towards me, mopping himself now with a huge handkerchief. "It gets the sugar going, you know. In the blood. You want a tomato?"

I nod my head, fearful. His little blue eyes grab at my legs. He takes my hand, his own slippery with sweat, and leads me into the greenhouse.

"Have what you like," he says. "Feel free." He closes the greenhouse door and pretends to potter with something, a watering can, raffia, I don't know. I reach out my hand for a tomato. He has sneaked up, this fat old man, behind me and suddenly plunges his face into my neck. All sweat and bristle, he laps at my neck as the Masai tribe drink at the necks of their cattle. Voracious for any liquid I am storing, he turns me (I have not yet picked the tomato), prises my lips open and drinks at my mouth, his tongue greedily searching for the last drop.

No, I don't cry for help. I don't try to resist him. Now my mouth is dry, I want the tomato more than ever. I am still holding the canvas bag, with its preparations for the pool. The sooner I can get to the pool the better. He takes the bag from me, puts it deliberately on the floor, sits down in an old basket chair that can hardly take his weight. When he pulls me onto his knee it sways perilously. From now on everything is accompanied by the protesting groans of the old chair.

First he rocks me; then his hand slides up under my smock; encountering pants, his fingers become troubled, searching here and there; at last, finding their way, they separate me; one stubby finger (nicotine stained, the nail black with earth, I imagine) probes relentlessly until it discovers an entrance. He is talking all the time, but quite unintelligibly. I am impaled on his finger, but when I look at his face it is not triumphant, the noble face of a conqueror; it is silly, sheepish, the face of a man caught doing wrong.

Disgust will make me cruel from now on. How I despise him. I get up (the chair is relieved), pull at my smock, pick up my bag. His penis, jutting out of those folds of grey, is fat and white as an unopened magnolia. He also stands, too ashamed to look me in the eye, and turns to reach for his collar and jacket. When he puts on the clerical collar, its black bib over the sweat-soaked shirt, I burst out of the greenhouse and start running running running

* * *

To the pool, straight to it with no hesitation, tearing off my smock on the way, out of my slippers and crash, smack onto the cold water, stomach smarting as I go under. Opening my eyes, I see Gondzik staring at me from above. But I swim deeper, huddling into the water. He descends with hair flying, beard still apparently dry, grabs me by the ankle and hauls me to the surface. As we break, a tangle of arms and legs, into the air, I can hear myself screaming and change the key of the scream so that it will sound like laughter. Various people sitting round the pool look appalled: we appear to be behaving like two-year-olds. I push away from the side, cast myself off and drift face upwards, weightless, the water lapping against my temples. Now all strange hours and all strange loves are over, dreams and desires and sombre songs and sweet. Now folds the lily all her sweetness up and slips into the bosom of the lake. Now drowns the gardener in the porphyry font. Now I know what to expect from the place, that it is full of traps and snares, one must be continually wary, water is the only innocent element. Slowly, very very slowly, I lay the memory to rest. It leaves me, sinking fathom after fathom into darkness. But I float like a cork, rocking in the wake of Gondzik's energetic crawl.

5

"Have you met anyone?" Gondzik asks casually.

"You mean from the outside? No." I have prepared myself for this, the lie is convincing.

Gondzik gets supplies sent from somewhere. He pours small measures of brandy into two plastic glasses. He gets his bed made every day (the rest of us only twice in a number of days) and has the confidence of a man with special privileges: of which he was once, or will be again, deprived?

"Have you?" I ask. After a long pause, studying the brown liquid in his glass, tipping it this way and that, he says, "No." We are both lying.

"I've seen a dog, though. Running about on the lawn."

"I know," I say. "It's mine."

"What makes you say that? This is a red setter."

"Then it can't be mine. Mine is a mongrel."

So I have suddenly appropriated a dog. I know (with a slight sense of dread—life is so much easier without responsibilities) that before long it will come bounding towards me down the pool path, throwing itself at me in an ecstasy of love, barking its head off. Once things begin to happen, they happen fast. For instance, I took an interminable time or at least a few moments trying to convince myself that I could avoid Gondzik, since I already knew him. But he stood patiently in my way and I have to get to know him very differently, without disturbing my memories or borrowing on my expectations of the future. So the dog, when it comes, will be a present dog, a dog of this place. I will be part of its life, but it will not be part of mine, not to begin with. Nevertheless, together with the sense of dread is a sense of pleasure. What a funny dog with its bat ears, head on one side, paw lifted, nose twitching from side to side from smell to smell: something to look forward to.

Gondzik's room is tricked out like a chapel, which some girl, in an excess of girlishness, has painted virgin white. All it lacks is muslin lifting and floating in the breeze from the fan. There is a white altar screen, white choir stalls, a white prie-dieu. Dark Gondzik doesn't suit it at all. He doesn't even know what a prie-dieu is for, or the hole in the (white) papal chair, unless it's a commode. Nevertheless he seems quite at ease in this setting, doesn't find it offensive.

"I hear he's going to have to resign."

"Who? The Director?"

"He won't make a statement. Says he's too busy laying out the tennis courts."

"Who told you?"

"Not that I'm against tennis courts, mind you. I like tennis."

"He's fiddling, you mean, while Rome burns."

"It's a question of where the money comes from. Otherwise tennis courts are perfectly valid, don't you think?"

"Who says what you hear?"

"Oh . . . people talk, you know."

"But if the Director resigns, will it make any difference? To us?"

"I shouldn't think so. They'll probably carry on with the tennis courts just the same."

"You mean corruption is inevitable?"

Narrowing his eyes, he seems to look into some distant cranny of time, perhaps into his own future. "Maybe."

The trouble with Gondzik (now) is that he has become an athletic intellectual. Life, particularly sex, has gone to his head. I have almost given up hope (if it was hope) of his body. At one time, I thought, he would drive into me with his eyes holding my face like a vice. We would stare each other out until we became entranced, our eyes locked together, absolutely thoughtless, in a state of shock. We worked slowly, with dedication, towards this miracle. Now he has so many thoughts, theories, speculations, conclusions, premises, data, analyses and propositions in his head that his flesh and skin have become insensitive. He thrashes water as though it has to be subdued; he attacks harmless games; he whacks the air, deafens it with noise for no apparent reason. He no longer conveys sweet messages from mouth to mouth, but bites and gnaws: again the dog image, the meatless bone, the begging. He talks about all women as girls, who are in constant supply; or perhaps it is their demand that is constant, since they are kept in a state of deprivation. If I said to him "Be still" he would laugh it off, forgetting, or not yet knowing, what stillness means.

He is, of course, equally hopeless about me, about my obsessions. He doubts whether I can be reclaimed. I have been unfaithful to him too often. He disapproves strongly (with all the ambivalent feelings of a father?) of my dreams about you, whether they are hostile or tender. I say that as far as dreams are concerned I am probably incurable, and may well be visited by you for the rest of my life. It seems to Gondzik that I am wilfully helpless in this respect. One good push and I could be rid of you entirely—why the flabbiness, the apathy, the passive acceptance? He uses the word "exorcise." You are to be "exorcised" by some means or other. But you know what? At this point, I can't be bothered. I have used so many means, struggled so hard, and the result is not entirely contemptible. My waking hours are undisturbed so long as I keep to the straight and narrow path—see what happens immediately I leave it—and avoid heights, precipices, quicksand, swamps, culs-de-sac, and regard every package and letter (perhaps some sort of ray machine, as they use at airports, would be wise) with reasonable suspicion. We are all so cluttered with restrictions anyway that it hardly matters. If I can't be a nun, I can at least steer myself towards some tolerable tropic clime where the chances of contentment are slightly above average for the time of year.

Naturally this would seem abominably dull and tepid to Gondzik. It does to me. But unlike Gondzik I know that survival is a long, hard slog from the amoeba upwards. In spite of his scorn, his impatience, I haven't done too badly. If I can survive an encounter with the gardener in bright daylight and with you in the unpredictable landscapes of my dreams, I can survive anything. Isn't that the point? One must always at all times be contained and defensive, rigidly abiding by one's own rules. I salute myself, without irony: doing well.

"I hear that three new people are coming," Gondzik says, adding gloomily, "All men."

"Have you been to the vegetable garden?" I will not be drawn back there, of course; but there is pleasure in casually introducing a forbidden subject into ordinary conversation.

"Where do they come from, why do they come, I've never heard of any of them."

"Perhaps you'd like to come with me one day. There are strawberries and peas, peaches, tomatoes."

"In winter there are very few people. They have wine at dinner." His hand moves idly to the table lamp, he pulls the chain, switching it on.

"You have been here in the winter. You have."

He looks puzzled; almost hurt, if this present Gondzik can be hurt. "Maybe."

"It was cold, very cold, your feet froze to the ground!"

He bats the air for silence, but I am momentarily possessed.

"The lake was frozen, you walked across it, she was skating cutting figures of eight, she was eight, wasn't she—"

"Her little skirt like daisy petals flung out from a yellow stem, she loves me, she loves me not—"

"You plucked them, leaving her shivering."

"GODDAMN YOU!"

He will probably hit me; but he doesn't; he breathes at me as he should breathe in the water, coming up for air; then he walks over to the papal chair, sits heavily, beard on chest.

I wish I could go on, but the inspiration, vision, whatever it was, is over. I have no idea what possessed me: no skating child in my experience, the lake has looked solid with slimy weed, but never frozen. He would have told me about it, surely, as we lay in bed or by the fire or in the meadow. I believe he told me everything, except what his analyst thought of me. Then perhaps the skating child who burst out of my mouth is part of my memory. He must have described her so accurately that, in my mind's eye at least, I have actually seen her. I am determined to go further, however risky it is.

"Do you remember how we met?"

"I don't remember," he says, repeating pat the rules, "I experience." I attack him with some tirade about sheepish obedience, accuse him of cowardice, of inertia, I venomously tell him that he bores me, is mediocre, a sissy-kisser, a teacher's pet, a conniver at fascism, a parasite, a sycophant. He is shaking with more and more laughter, a man watching some incredibly comic antic. I am entertaining him, for God's sake. I throw myself down on the floor, drum the floor with my heels, twist and turn while some part of me quite calmly waits for the result. There is no result. He is speechless with laughter. Tear-smeared, exhausted, I get up and stagger into a corner, stand in the corner. A grown woman and I can't get what I want, a simple agreement.

"There's no point in being here," he says at last, sober again, "if you don't go along with it, obey the rules as you say. It's one of the few situations which one can quite validly call a waste of time. Why don't you leave?"

"Leave?"

"Of course. There's nothing to stop you."

"But where would I go?"

He shrugs. "I don't know. Back to all that, I suppose."

"All what?"

"The obsessions. The loneliness you have described."

"Have I described loneliness?"

"Of course. It's easy to avoid meeting people out there."

"But there are millions of people out there." Now I am the one repeating what I have been told. I am sure I've never seen millions of people. Maybe I've seen a dozen, and a dog.

"Are you sure you haven't met anyone here?"

I am a bad liar when caught off my guard. My lies have to be carefully constructed, with a basis of truth. Therefore I prefer not to answer this question, or rather to parry it with a sullen "You."

"Then why ask me if I remember how we met?"

"All right. You're cleverer than I am."

"No. I expect I've been here longer. That's all."

The smugness of it. I'll go back to my motionless journeys, an armchair traveller to every place under the sun, including the moon; I'll speculate about bathrooms and nineteenth-century poets and whether worms have teeth, like the Duchess of Newcastle (a kindred spirit wherever she is). The most I can hope for, it seems, is to be a clown tumbling through my own hoops.

"Time you grew up a little," Gondzik says quietly, standing close to me. "You need to forget all that."

"All what?" But already, over the space of a few seconds, I have no idea what he means.

He holds me by the shoulders and moves me a little

nearer to the light. "We'll make something of you yet. Take a good look at me."

I do. I look hard. I realise that it was not me whom Gondzik nailed down with those little flickering eyes; he has never rolled and expostulated in the middle of a meadow with *me*. It happened with someone else. I, not Gondzik, am the stranger.

It is very curious to begin with, as I stand looking at him. I feel myself rocking on my feet, losing balance. I am not who I thought I was. I am literally no longer myself. I have no past, but am doing everything for the first time. This is where I begin. Memory, if it ever existed, is irretrievably drowned. Gondzik has never met me before. I didn't lose my way when I went to the vegetable garden, there was no way to lose. I was guided there by official directions. I must obey official directions, there is no alternative.

Gondzik nods, and switches off the light. I don't feel at all foolish as I ask him how I am to get back to my room. He, not finding the question foolish, accompanies me.

6

From now on it is all (briefly) less confusing. I sit still in my rocking chair, my mind is blank, I make no journeys. Gondzik is simply Gondzik, I'm no longer curious about overheard remarks. The tree is a tree, the lily pond a lily pond, the bushes are bushes. When the red setter runs across the lawn, he is a red setter running across the lawn. I don't look forward, and I don't look back. Since I don't dream, I don't remember my dreams, or the other way round (a little rocky here). In any case, at this time you no longer exist for me; whether you exist for other people is a matter of no importance. I am, you are, he is: that's the lesson. I study it doggedly. My light brackets shine much brighter, I've noticed.

For the first time, I take a straightforward interest in the others, even going so far as to memorise some of their names. Elizabeth just happens to stand in an attitude I would once have called dejected. Paul smiles because that is the way his face is. The anthropologist, Hermann, is an anthropologist. Revlon is a man who says that he deciphers messages from the ground. The tiny woman with cropped hair and a face like a marmoset (Rowena) is a tiny woman with a face like a marmoset. Now you ask how do I know what a marmoset is? I don't. It's one of the many words I've learned by heart. Words are words. Their meanings are their meanings. And so on.

I am now included much more in the community. I have become one of Them. I still don't understand everything they say, but I accept everything they say: I met my mother in the rose garden, I will be meeting my son outside the garage, my aunt is coming to the pool. Very advanced stuff, this: hard to grasp, for a beginner. I can get as far as "I am eating my hash" and they nod graciously, congratulating me. I am very proud. I am given an ornamental card, stars on a blue background, "With Best Wishes from the Director": handwritten, the "r" coming back on itself and making an emphatic line underneath that august title.

Also I am now entrusted to pass on more important rumours than what day of the week it is: Hathaway is out, Rogers is in, but Hathaway says that Phillips knew all the time and Rogers says that Phillips' evidence is invalid since he no longer acts in an official capacity, therefore Hathaway is in again and Rogers out. I become as nifty at these (still meaningless) messages as a blind girl at a loom. Dickens (I have begun to read the books) tells me that blind girls are nifty at looms. That is how I know.

I feel vaguely sorry for the three new men, I don't (of course) know why. They huddle together, huddling together. Only Gondzik has introduced himself to them so far, and hasn't told me their names. Anyway I'm not at all interested. Until they learn the rules, they are irrelevant.

One morning, after dark, I actually stumble on the source, one of the sources, of the rumours. I have come up from breakfast as usual, directly they have finished ringing the bell (which tells us when to finish breakfast). But I am astounded to find a member of the staff still in my room. She is flicking a duster about quite uselessly. I hesitate in the doorway. "Come in, dear," she says, flicking with even more energy. Then, in exactly the same tone of voice, "They're having him up in front of the Committee, my what a lot of bottles you have, well, I'll be seeing you, cheerio for now," and she goes out, flicking the duster under her arm; but at the door she turns and winks hugely, screwing up the whole side of her face.

I am thrown into a bit of a fluster. What to do? I have been entrusted with an original rumour (a great honour), but it seems to leap about in my hands like a freshly caught trout (Dickens). Should I tell Gondzik, or throw it casually into the conversation at dinner? What do the rules say? But silly me, there are no rules about spreading rumours which concern the office. There cannot be a rule to deal with the possibility that *the office itself is breaking the rules.* I don't know what's the matter with me.

So I take the little book of directions that Gondzik has thoughtfully provided me with, and go to his room. I knock, he calls "Yes?" which may or may not mean permission to enter. I take the risk. He is looking out of his window through a pair of binoculars. "Hi," he says, without un-gluing his eyes. I sit down, avoiding the papal chair because it looks uncomfortable. After a while he puts the binoculars on the table, asking "What's up?"

"Nothing." I'm very casual.

"I thought you were studying."

"It's too hot."

He smiles, ruffling my hair. "Can't have you backsliding, you know. By the way, the courts are pretty well finished. Do you play?"

"Play?"

"Tennis."

Now how do I know whether I play tennis or not? I make a shot in the dark. "No."

"Pity. Maybe one of the new men plays tennis."

Suddenly he throws something across the room, a pencil, it lands just by my foot. I know it is a signal. Bending to pick it up, I say "They're having him up in front of the Committee"; then handing it to him, "Your pencil."

"Who told you?" he murmurs, staring out of the window.

"A housekeeper."

"Which one?"

"The fat one with the butterfly glasses."

"Mavis." He turns, comes over to me, traces my jaw with his finger. "You're looking quite pretty today. I like that."

I have an impulse to squat down, put my head on one side, hold up my paws: to be rewarded. Impulses must be avoided at all costs. Wait for the order. Following the directions again, I go back to my room to wait.

* * *

It must be perfectly clear by now that, for all my efforts, I am recounting many things which are over, or which seem to me to be over. I feel quite safe, now, in saying that this period of my stay seems to me to have been exceptionally dull. Imagine being without associations or memory, totally without a sense of time. Imagine the banality of a tree being no more than a tree. Imagine not feeling pain, let alone not understanding it. Imagine being without whims or curiosity. Imagine being a blank slate, an empty glass. Looking back on this stage (I have no idea how long it lasted, and perhaps it was necessary) there seem to have been few incidents of even the slightest significance. Mostly I learned names (like marmoset), passed on messages, sat in my rocking chair, slept dreamlessly (I thought) and avoided going out except, occasionally, in the company of Gondzik. He seemed pleased with me, but no longer touched me. If I saw him from my window wandering across the lawn with his arm round a girl, I would merely think there is Gondzik wandering across the lawn with his arm round a girl.

There were sometimes screams in the night, but I simply told myself, "Someone is screaming." I waited to be directed to the vegetable garden again, but no directions came. There were storms, there was rain, the distant gardens shrouded in a mist of rain. The three new men, Simon, Dominic and George, were established. Dominic, being almost blind, learned the ropes before either of the others and was soon promoted to our company. As his hearing was very acute, Revlon sometimes gave him the job of listening for signals. The listening seemed to put him in a state of trance: looking straight ahead with his blind eyes he would recite messages in a low monotone, often hardly audible—we are having chicken for dinner, the Director has a cold, Hathaway is being blamed for everything, Mrs. Hathaway has attempted suicide, Hathaway has been cleared by new evidence which proves that the Director was in the Bahamas on the night in question, Milton is being blamed for everything, the chicken will be fried, Mrs. Hathaway is dead. Dominic became a kind of oracle.

Mavis, the housekeeper, visited me frequently. Insofar as I was capable of emotion during this period, I became quite fond of her. She was not particularly interested in the office dramas (she cleaned for some very minor assistant to an assistant, who seemed to know less than we did about it all), but she had a rich fund of stories about her husband's gout, the inefficiency of the supermarket, her married daughter's obstetrical troubles, the movie she saw last night. They were to me, you understand, fairy stories. I had a feeling they probably weren't allowed but, receiving no direction on this point, continued to listen to them with a faint twinge of what passed for guilt. In fact I looked forward to them, which in itself was reprehensible. All the time she talked, she flicked, knocking over bottles, making the pastoral engraving always more askew so that before long I would have had to lie on the floor to look at it, if I had wanted to look at it. When conversation failed (as it often did in those days) I would tell Gondzik a few of Mavis's stories and he always listened with the greatest attention.

It must have been about now that they made the bold experiment (which was to prove so significant) of getting the entertainers in. I suppose the money for this, too, came from the Repair Fund. Perhaps it was intended to distract us from our interest (it had to leak out somehow) in the affairs of the office. God knows that I, at least, had nothing else to be interested in. All that happened to me was that I sat in a deck chair, like the others, and watched small people dancing about at the end of lawn, in front of the lily pond. Either they danced or they strutted about, wearing peculiar clothes, or sometimes they stood still. As the authorities (so we were told) had been unable to afford microphones or loudspeakers, all this was dumb-show and not in the least distracting. I hadn't any idea what they were talking or singing about, if they were talking or singing, or what their whimsical dances were meant to represent. The orchestra was slightly preferable: thin sounds of music did, occasionally, drift to us from the sawing and blowing ants on their little gilt chairs. But as the place is (for some reason, possibly an endowment) equipped with an excellent stereo player and a library of records, the introduction of these minute musicians seemed a little unnecessary. However, we all attended the performances, and when they appeared to be over we clapped enthusiastically.

It was during one of these concerts—Rachmaninov, I think—that I saw the gardener again. Collarless, in the same striped shirt, he came out of the trees behind the lily pond and stood for a while, apparently listening. I registered this in my usual way, without comment and without any positive reaction. I knew that he had assaulted me, but not the meaning of the word; in the same way that I knew the way to Gondzik's room, but without his directions wouldn't have known how to get there. The gardener leaned on the low wall, cupped his hand into the green lily water and appeared to drink. Then he lumbered back into the trees, fitting the description of a solitary bear. I neither missed him nor expected to see him again.

I don't think I am concealing anything about this period. It had a beginning, in Gondzik's room; and owing to this bold introduction of entertainment it came to an end, or was at least halted. Perhaps it will come back, but I hope not. I think I would rather be killed than die of my own accord. Then at least somebody else would be responsible for my lifelessness; it would be in some way a shared experience.

7

There had been (this is still recollection) many days of
rain and mist, the air, if it could be called air, swampy
and foetid. I didn't go to the pool, though Gondzik did,
rain or shine. Most people stayed indoors, sitting about in
the lounges and waiting rooms turning over the leaves of
books, growing heavier and heavier. Lively mosquitoes
swarmed against the screens, hungry for blood. Lamps
were left on in the corridors and on the landings. The
space between breakfast and dinner became immeasurable. We were really being put through it.

They should have brought the entertainers indoors, but
this was apparently not allowed, so the entertainers were
given leave of absence while the bad weather lasted. The
deck chairs were stacked on the terrace below my window, not reminding me of wet summers in Folkestone or
Hayling Island. Revlon stated that it was August, but
nobody cared. He became pettish and retired to his room,
leaving Dominic to listen as best he could to floors and
walls, which told him very little.

About the middle of one of these attenuated days I
noticed faint shadows on the lawn beneath the trees and
bushes. The mist was glaring, the heat almost intolerable.
The deck chairs began to steam. Splinters of sunlight fell

here and there and at last the sun itself cracked through, the damp stone sizzled. After a while people crept out onto the terrace, singly, in twos and threes, looking about them as though emerged from the hold of an ark. Gondzik appeared in white sport shirt and trousers, the legs tapered as they used to be in the sixties, the top of his head (seen by me) slightly balding. They fanned out over the lawn, inspecting, investigating, Gondzik a player going out to bat, making swinging movements with clasped hands.

Something moved in me, lurched, lightened. I went to my vast cupboard and was surprised to find most of my clothes heaped in a corner, unfit to wear. I looked at myself in my three mirrors, one after another. A porridge face looked back, eyes dead as raisins, mouth dragged down, hair lifeless. I looked at my slumping body, grown into the mould of the rocking chair. My arms seemed to be covered in fine grey ash; my toenails were broken, there was stubble in my armpits. I knew I was not a pretty sight, but as yet didn't draw any conclusions. There I (presumably) was. But I didn't want to go down and join the others, I knew that. I rejoined the rocking chair and watched the lawn.

I am as bad at calculating distance as time; all I can say is that the lily pond, with its low wall and supplicating (it looks supplicating) statue is so far from my window that I have to narrow my eyes to see it clearly. The lawn slopes all the way from the house to the lily pond, uninterrupted except for a cluster of three trees. The terrace in front of the house, therefore, might as well be the back row of an enormous stadium: one would need binoculars to see the lily pond in detail. I hadn't questioned why I saw the gardener, during the Rachmaninov, so sharply.

That day, as the others were making a kind of broken wave approaching the pond, Gondzik in the lead, the wave faltered, scattered and turned on itself; it now rolled back towards the terrace, Gondzik in the rear looking (I registered) a little downcast. Minute people had arrived at the pond carrying planks and poles and what looked like prefabricated wooden structures. They swarmed about, the sound of hammering so distant that it might have been a woodpecker in a tree, a solitary cricket. They worked fast, men and possibly women in blue jeans, some naked to the waist. Very soon the lily pond was surrounded, and hidden by this high, circular, wooden wall. It was impossible to tell what was going on behind it.

The others seemed to be excited. As they came up the steps, some of them looked backwards; others, having reached the terrace, peered from beneath shading hands. A lot of speculation was going on. Gondzik moved here and there in his sporty white, wearing dark glasses. The bell sounded for dinner, and for the first time I wasn't ready.

I put something on, brushed my hair and found my way to the stairs by means of the pocketbook. I steadied myself on the oak bannister while going down the stairs, as it seemed I was unaccustomed to walking. In the dining room, I joined the end of the queue, shuffled forward with no particular prospect except that of having something in my mouth, chewing and swallowing. When I saw the plate sparsely covered with meat and vegetables I sat down in the nearest chair and ate until the plate was clean. I realised from the chatter that we were going to have some rather special entertainment, a treat after our long deprivation. The news, apparently, had been posted on the notice board. I never looked at the notice board, partly because it was usually empty and partly because even if there were anything on it the message would not be addressed to me personally, it would merely be some general announcement or possibly new rule or warning.

When the bell sounded, I took my plate into the kitchen with the others; then I drifted with them, idly enough, onto the terrace. The deck chairs were still stacked. The edifice, whatever it was, round the lily pond seemed to be finished, no one to be seen. Gondzik, passing hurriedly, said "How are you," but it wasn't a question. He ran down the steps to the lawn and we followed him. We did not form a wave this time, but a ragged line. I was carried along, I think, with no intention or anticipation, towards the wall. When we got near enough and were actually filing through an opening, I saw that it was made of great sheets of hardboard with numbers stamped on the back, held together with wooden struts so new that they were still jagged with splinters.

* * *

Once inside, we see that the wall forms more of an arc than a circle, there are rough, tiered benches placed like steps from the top of the wall down to the ground. There are fourteen aisles radiating down through the top eight rows of benches to a semi-circular wooden walk (or promenade); below this only six aisles through shorter rows of benches (but eight rows just the same), the whole enclosing the lily pond, over which are lights sweeping to and fro with white beams. In the front row of this lower and smaller semi-circle is an open box draped in sombre purple and containing three or four of the pseudo-Jacobean chairs from the dining room. Behind the lily pond they have erected a wooden platform, backed and winged by three walls, the side walls opening outwards like welcoming arms towards the auditorium (which I now know, or even possibly recognise it to be). I climb up the steep steps of the nearest aisle, having to raise my knees high as I do so, and sit down in an unostentatious (hiding) place in the back semi-circle. Although it is still light, the arc lamps sweep down the tiered benches as though to search someone out.

There is a murmur of voices sounding expectant: close your eyes and it might be a crowd of twenty thousand instead of this meagre handful. Young people carrying a strange assortment of instruments arrive and sit on the grass between the lily pond and the platform: I can see bagpipes, a violin and 'cello, an accordion, a drum; now a flute, and a girl with a huge pair of cymbals. They blow and saw and pipe and clash with no co-ordination but very quietly, as though under the sea, each absorbed in his or her own sound.

Now a man carried a bed onto the platform, so light it must be made of aluminium, its mattress and bedclothes attached. He places it on the right-hand side of the platform, goes away, comes back with a similar bed which he places about three feet from the first one, goes again, returns with another: three beds side by side. In a moment he comes back with a chair and a large carton of sorts, but there is a commotion along the benches and my attention is distracted. Two strangers, a man and a woman, are entering the purple-shrouded box. They are both in evening dress of the formal, slightly old-fashioned style worn by royalty. They bow (though no one has applauded) and the man raises his hand in a kind of greeting gesture. When they are seated, two or three more people slip in behind them like shadows. I lean towards Dominic, sitting two rows down, placid with his blind stare.

"Who are they?"

"The Director and his wife."

"My goodness."

I sit back, absorbing the sight of the Director and his wife. How extraordinary of them, in the middle of their troubles, to be seen. Or perhaps that's the point. My wits are being sharpened like arrows, all sorts of unusual movements are stretching and exercising my muscles. By now the platform is almost furnished. As the last touch, the stagehand carries in a huge cellophane window with pelmet and curtains attached and props it against the back wall. He nods curtly to the Director (a disbeliever grumpily passing in front of an altar) and goes away, leaving the stage set.

The ill-assorted orchestra strikes up, all instrumentalists together on the beat. Surprisingly, it is a pleasant sound. I notice the Director take spectacles out of his breast pocket, polish them on a white handkerchief, latch them behind his ears. The arc lamps go out, leaving the whole place in twilight but for an underwater lamp cunningly concealed in the lily pond which lights and shadows the statue. The orchestra stops with a clash of cymbals, the platform is flooded with daylight, a large dog enters, bows gravely to the Director, and begins to act.

The dog trots here and there on the stage, then exits. A woman comes on, wearing a blue robe; she moves across the stage with decorous power, her calm face illuminated from within. Suddenly she stops, alert, and turns to the cellophane window. Behind the window we (and the woman) momentarily see the face of a devil or king, rakishly crowned with thorns. I imagine this to be a kind of prologue, as on the terrified cry "My children!" the face disappears and the woman rushes offstage, criminally assaulted by fear.

I am very disturbed by this cry, and can't really concentrate on the next scene, which concerns the dog, the woman, a clown, two male actors and a chorus dressed in practice tights and leotards so old that they seem to have been chewed by rats. The Chorus is telling us that danger lurks behind the window (which we know) and that the woman's great fear is justified. The dog howls dreadfully. The clown takes no notice, but struts about in pompous attitudes, making the audience laugh. How can they laugh, with that terror about to reveal itself any moment? "My children! My children!" The clown drags the dog away, the two male actors get into separate beds, the chorus walks lithely off on the balls of its feet. The woman is left wringing her hands, putting a brave face on it.

FIRST MALE ACTOR   Is anything there?
          WOMAN   All quite quiet and still. Oh, how I
     wish I was not going out to dinner tonight.
SECOND MALE ACTOR   Can anything harm us, mother, after
     the night-lights are lit?
          WOMAN   Nothing, precious. They are the eyes
     a mother leaves behind her to guard her children.

On this, the lights slowly fade. It is not yet dark enough, however, in the auditorium for me not to notice figures scurrying about. Suddenly the cymbals crash, making me jump off the bench with terror: spotlit, the demon king stands in an arrogant attitude, his thorn crown askew on long black hair, his narrow body gleaming, hairless and slender as a girl, thighs clenched with power. He is, I suppose, some age of child or possibly adolescent. After lingering in his spotlit glory for perhaps one second too long, he carries on with the play.

The third bed, we now see, is occupied. The woman of the first scene, who by rights should now be out to dinner, makes a great to-do of sitting up, stretching, yawning and so on. She merely smiles when the King asks her this rather senseless question:

KING Woman, what have I to do with you?
WOMAN More than you think.

Smiling, she holds out her arms to him. Smiling, the King steps back. Smiling, she gets out of bed, ruthlessly pursuing him with outstretched arms.

KING *Noli me tangere.*
WOMAN Why not?
KING Because you are my mother.
WOMAN (*smiling*) Absolute rubbish. (*Aside*) Nay, what should mortal fear, for whom the decrees of Fortune are supreme, and who hath clear foresight of nothing? 'Tis best to live at random, as one may. (*Maternally, to King*) But fear not thou touching wedlock with thy mother. Many men ere now have so fared in dreams also: but he to whom these things are of nought bears his life most easily.
KING Is that right? Really?
WOMAN Of course.

And of course the woman is lying. The King turns his back on her.

KING Come with me.
WOMAN Oh dear, I mustn't. Think of the children. Besides, I can't fly.
KING But you are an angel.
WOMAN Naturally.

56

I am distracted from the dialogue between the King and
the woman (which was interesting enough) by the crank-
ing and clattering of some huge machine, a kind of crane
or derrick, that puts its head over the back wall like an
inquisitive dinosaur, nosing back and forth. At the same
time a tall, rather stout man wearing a barrister's wig and
gown clambers with difficulty (because, as we soon realise,
he is blind) onto the platform. He looks vaguely familiar to
me, and as he turns his sightless stare upon the auditorium
I cringe back on my bench, not wishing to be recognised.
Stately, he turns and confronts the King, who seems to
have finished nagging and being nagged by the woman for
the moment.

BARRISTER   You are a blind man, Your Majesty, who now
   has sight?
   KING   Never.
BARRISTER   Then might I put to you that you are a beggar
   who is now rich?
   KING   No.
BARRISTER   You will make your way to a strange land, then,
   feeling before you with your staff. Kindly think about
   the question and don't answer off the top of your head.
The King crows like a cock, an excellent imitation.
BARRISTER   Would you mind repeating that, sir?
   KING   I want always to be a little boy and to have fun.
BARRISTER   The future will come of itself, though I shroud
   it in silence.
   KING   Shroud it, then. (*He is devastated with his own
   wit.*)
BARRISTER   You are found at once brother and father of the
   children with whom you consort—am I right? Son and
   husband of the woman who bore you—am I right? Heir
   to your father's bed and shedder of your father's blood
   —correct?
   KING   No one is going to catch me, lady, and make me
   a man. I will never go near my parents! Who is this old
   fellow, anyway? Get him to a cloister!

Members of the chorus run forward with supple joints, lift the old Barrister bodily and carry him shoulder-high off the stage, waving his brief like a flag of surrender. In the general hubbub the two male actors have slipped out of bed and joined the woman underneath the great machine, which has cables dangling from its mouth. It is only later, with a lurch of the stomach such as one feels when watching trapeze artists, that I realise the actors have in some way attached themselves to these cables.

KING Bring your brats with you, if you must. (*The male actors cringe slightly.*) I'll teach you how to jump on the wind's back and then away we go. Mother, when you are sleeping in your silly bed you might be flying about with me, saying funny things to the stars.

The woman is obviously infatuated.

WOMAN My darling boy.

KING And you can tell me stories about naughty children who have to be spanked when they do wrong.

WOMAN I will, I will.

The King has cunningly fastened himself to the remaining cable. The window, by some theatrical trickery, has opened wide on the real night, punctured with stars. The King calls commandingly, "Now come!" and a little less light than thistledown he, the woman and the two male actors are hauled into the air and swung out into the woods beyond, the machine creaking dreadfully. A dog howls, the sound taken up by the bagpipes. The window gapes. Somewhat flustered, but nevertheless convincing, the woman reappears, wringing her hands and calling "My children! My children!" But, as we all know, they have left her, perhaps never to return.

* * *

When the lights go up I am weeping terribly and, as I realise in a few moments, with some noise. I stuff something, possibly the skirt of my dress, into my mouth, cramming the grief inside. Through my streaming eyes I see the Director chatting to his wife. He glances round, sees me, leans backwards to say a few words to one of his aides. The aide nods, taking my number. I am so alone. Gondzik hurries along the diazoma, presumably on his way to the bar. They have even thought of a bar. I am cruelly presented with everything I ever knew about Gondzik from long before those distant days when we walked round the lake and he saw the skater. I feel, as someone who is touched by a ghost, his tenderness and passion. He used to come whenever I asked for help, or demanded it. Why does he hurry now, beard curving and pointing upwards, pretending he has no time? After my period of numbness I am desperately vulnerable. Every reaction, every response and secretion and blocked feeling is working to make up for lost time. Time lost, time wasted? The Director's aide's wife is looking at me in the mirror of her powder compact while she pretends to jab at her nose. She says something out of the corner of her mouth to the aide, who leans forward and murmurs in the Director's ear. The Director nods. The lights dim again in mosquito-infested darkness: they dance demented in the stream of the spotlight and I wonder whether I can slip away, but know it is impossible. Where would I go? Besides, the play has started again.

The Chorus appears and intones some prophecy of woe: as far as I can gather, the woman will die horribly because she is going to live with her children; the King will plead ignorance of the whole affair and go off to dally with (my heart jumps) Red Indians; there will be bloodshed and pain. Sure enough, when the Chorus pirouettes away the woman is lying apparently lifeless, an arrow in her navel. She is naked, one knee drawn up, arms flung about her head. A group of male actors (including the original two) stand round her in triumphant attitudes. They slap each other on the back, rock with soundless laughter, zipping up their flies and rearranging their shirts. One of them stubs out his cigar on the woman's thigh, another kicks her with his shiny boot. It is very unpleasant, for as far as I can see she has done them no harm. The King appears, with the usual accompaniment of cymbals and a cowering squaw. He is disgusted with the whole scene (as I am) and commands a shrine to be built. The actors obediently run about with shrine-building materials and finally inter the woman. But no sooner have they done so than lo, she rises immaculate from the shrine, clothed once more in the blue robe, a light shining behind her graceful head.

WOMAN   Where am I?
MALE ACTOR   Goddess, for you we built this shrine.
WOMAN   Thank you so much.
MALE ACTOR   And we are your children.
OMNES   (*kneeling with outstretched arms*)   Goddess, be our mother!
WOMAN   Ought I? You see I'm only a little girl. I have no real experience.
OMNES   Age cannot wither you nor custom stale your infinite variety.
WOMAN   It's true I can cook.
KING   That'll do for the time being.

Exalted, the woman holds out her arms. All the male actors (except the King) move into her arms, lay their heads on her breasts so that she is practically submerged. The King (who cannot, because of some ancient curse, be touched) sulks briefly, then exits with Minnehaha. The woman, invisible now beneath the nuzzling actors, calls, "Father!" The cry is taken up on tape, relayed round the auditorium: "Father! Father!" in an ever-increasing volume of anguish. At last it is stifled, the stage blacks out to the accompaniment of sucking noises, all the actors having lollipops hidden in their sleeves.

During the intermission, pretending to be calm, I am impatient for the reappearance of the King. I have fallen in love with him, of course: his grace, his strength, his arrogance, his invulnerability, his maddening conceit. What a man he is, this manless wonder. At the same time my arms, too, long to be filled. My arms cry out down to the palms of my hands. This time the Director turns right round in his seat to stare at me. The aide is asking whether I should be thrown out or requested to leave. The Director shakes his head, settling back in his chair. His wife seems to have no opinions at all; she has folded her program into a fan and is fanning herself fussily. I simply cannot do the right thing; even if I knew what the right thing was, I couldn't do it. Those who cannot conform are condemned to be ostracised. I positively do not know how to be a member of the audience, and since I don't know how to act (the mere thought of it terrifies me) there is really no place for me anywhere. Oh God, it's all a hopeless mis-understanding, but we must go through with it, the exits are blocked and there's no alternative.

So imagine my disappointment when the clown appears, pretending to be a dog, scurrying round the stage on all fours, lifting his leg against the furniture, while the on-lookers whoop with relief and hilarity. Mine, I know, is the only straight face in the house. I try to lift its contours, even if I can't smile. Gondzik's roars deafen me. Is it possible I don't get the point? Even Dominic is grinning. Is it so funny to be a dog, to be a man pretending to be a dog? It seems to me infinitely sad. With a final "woof, woof" the idiot goes off and we see the woman sitting in a chair in a forlorn attitude. This is more like it. "You have suffered too severely," Gondzik says again and again, "and will interfere with my mirth." But my mirth is frequently let loose, and I hope it doesn't contain cruelty. I can laugh, ha ha, at the simplest of jokes. Derision, however, is some-thing I do with a poker face and a whipping tongue, very far from comedy. I prefer to make other people laugh than to laugh myself: in that way I use ridicule, but am not expected myself to find it humourous.

Anyway, the woman is sitting in a forlorn attitude which —unlike the human dog—I recognise. The window is back in place (open), so it is obvious that she is mourning her fly-away children. In fact they come running through the door, as the machine is being reserved for another purpose. The woman jumps up with a cry of delight—but where is the King? Suddenly he appears, enthroned in a kind of open cabin on top of the crane. He raises his face to the spotlight, my darling, and with absolute horror I see that his eyes are gouged out, his face a mess of blood, iris and pupil. The woman shrieks and runs towards the window, possibly to throw herself out. The King's voice cracks as he speaks, descending momentarily into a deep bass.

KING They make me do this, for some reason. I've never been touched, so I don't know why. However, it's only makeup.

He wipes his face with a paper towel which he then throws carelessly into the wings. He stands up in the cabin (swaying dangerously) and is gold all over, a Midas who has touched himself, his long gold hair streaming from the fillet of golden thorns.

WOMAN (*aghast*) You are leaving me!
   KING Naturally. It would be unnatural to stay.
  MALE ACTORS But we are staying!
   KING That's none of my business. I am a golden boy, as you can see. It's inconvenient in some ways, but there it is, we must cut the umbilical cord and untie the Gordian knot. Away, away, on the back of the wind!

The machine makes a convulsive movement and he almost loses his balance. The woman calls up to him with beseeching hands.

WOMAN What time will you be back?
KING I don't know. Around one or seven.
WOMAN I'll have something ready for you, I'll have something ready . . .
KING (*being carried away*) Don't bother.
WOMAN I'll kill the golden calf!
KING I'll probably grab a sandwich . . .

As he is swung out of sight, an awful cockcrow resounds through the theatre. The lights dim. The woman stands very still, empty-handed. The male actors silently disperse, to be replaced by the Chorus. Apparently the Chorus has made a mistake or forgotten its lines; anyway, after brief and inaudible muttering it goes away. The woman stands very still, empty-handed.

* * *

Mrs. April and a male colleague come for me as I am caught up in the jostle of the escaping crowd: just a hand under my elbow, a voice in my ear.

"Not for long," they say.

"But is it a punishment?"

"Of course not. Just a change of scene."

"And will I be able to go back to my room soon?"

"Of course. Very soon."

"Will you tell Gondzik, Basil Gondzik?"

"Yes, we'll tell him."

"Is it far?"

"Not far at all."

"Will there be other people?"

"Of course there will."

So, held firmly by the elbows, I skim across the dark grass while the others are climbing the steps to the terrace outside the lighted house. I fancy I can see a light in my windows. Just before we enter the trees I twist my head round and look towards the theatre. They are already pulling it down, attacking recalcitrant rivets and bolts with hatchets.

PART TWO

8

When it is light again I look around me, raising myself on my elbows to see where I am: in a large bed in a large room. The other side of the bed is still warm (but I didn't dream, that I can remember). A cupboard gapes open, showing piles of shoes and clothes hanging anyhow. Every chair is hidden under accumulated clothes. On top of the chest of drawers (dull with dust) a drift of old letters curling at the edges, used envelopes, yellowing newspapers. I can see myself (though dimly, behind a mist of dust) in the dressing-table mirrors, which are triple. The dressing table is cluttered with unstoppered bottles, topless jars: when I examine it more closely I will find rubber bands, safety pins, hair grips, stained pieces of cotton wool, grimy tissues, empty tins of hair spray, bottles of nail varnish set solid with age, twenty miniature brushes caked with mascara, half a dozen pencils, a hairbrush solid with dirty hairs, two combs with missing teeth. . . . Thank god I haven't yet examined it, but am looking at the window: half the curtain hooks are missing, so that the grubby curtains hang in dolorous loops; one of the sash cords is broken. Why have they brought me to this terrible slum? I suppose I must try to clean it up. I swing energetically out of bed and look for something to put on. A grey towelling dressing gown has been thrown on the floor. I put it on with some distaste, finding a used, dried-up sanitary towel in the pocket. What kind of people live in this place, for God's sake?

The door once had a bolt, which has been ripped off. There is also a jagged hole in the bottom panel. Somebody kicked and kicked the door, I realise, when it was bolted, breaking both the bolt and the door. Maybe it's a lunatic asylum, but do I deserve this merely by weeping at a play? I creep out onto a landing, which is thick with the ammoniac smell of old urine. Through an open door I see children spread-eagled and curled in beds and cots, soaking in the warmth of saturated sheets. The chaos is indescribable; I can't encompass it; I don't understand how so many useless objects, so much dead matter, can accumulate in one place. I creep down the stairs on bare feet, tripping over a loose stair rod. Seeing the front door, I think of escape; but, as always, cannot believe in an alternative. Also I know that for reasons of their own (mine not to reason why) they have set me a Herculean task: I am to make order, find a place for everything and put everything in its place. The thought exhilarates and terrifies me. Perhaps they think I am the only one who can do it. I will make a detailed list and work my way through it item by item, slow and steady, not overtiring myself, taking care to eat properly and sleep well, but labouring quietly on until the job is finished. First, however, I will look at the basement.

I haven't bothered with the kitchen or the sitting room, knowing by now what I shall find. But I am unprepared for the basement. To begin with, it is dark. I stumble against what seem to be dozens of wheels, setting them spinning. When at last I find the light switch I see a tangle of bicycles, some without handlebars, nearly all without chains, a funeral pile of dead bicycles; also a couple of broken strollers and an old pram full of rubbish. I realise that I have no idea how to get rid of such things, the dustman won't take them. I open a door and a hundred, two hundred, shoes fall down on me; laced shoes, strapped shoes, sandals, slippers, dancing pumps with elastic to go round the ankle, muddy shoes, new shoes, wellington boots, football boots, plimsolls. . . . I gather up an armful and try to cram them back and shut the door, but now the landslide has been set in motion it is impossible, so I leave them, making a mental note to put the organisation and arrangement of shoes high on my list.

The next room, which leads out to a bedraggled garden, must be a nursery or playroom, the cupboard doors haven't been shut for years, the floor is ankle-deep in broken toys and ripped paper. I am past surprise, but not past caring. Passages crammed with litter lead off the main corridor, but I'm not going to investigate them yet or I may get confused and hopeless. I try a last door, and find it locked, either locked or boarded up. I've seen enough, anyway, and climb back to the ground floor.

Some unwashed, dishevelled children (I haven't washed, or brushed my hair either) are waiting for breakfast. I find half a dozen packets of cereal, with maybe a cupful of cereal in each; a bowl of hardened sugar; four saucers of butter, melted and set again. Somehow they get their breakfast. The fridge will have to be defrosted, the cupboards cleared out, the cooker scoured, the dishes washed up, the floor scrubbed.

"I can't find my tennis racquet and if I go without it they will send me home, so where is my tennis racquet?"

"My overall isn't marked and they say if I go once more with an unmarked overall they will send me home, so will you mark it?"

"I have lost my gym shoes."

"I have lost my French grammar."

"You stole my pen."

"I did not steal your pen."

"I haven't got any socks, someone's taken my socks."

"I feel sick."

"I need a loop on my swimming towel to hang it up with."

"I have lost my library book, will you write me a note?"

The racquet, the overall, the gym shoes, the grammar, the pen, the socks, the loop, the library book, the note: when they leave the kitchen (and presumably the house) they are more or less equipped. It isn't good enough. They should be completely equipped. The house is silent. I wait in some fear for somebody else to arrive. A baby begins to cry, so I go upstairs to see to it.

In fact the baby is relatively rewarding. I feed it, and it is fed. I wash it, and it is clean. I show it affection, it is contented. I am sorry to leave it, clean and tidy, in its pram (making sure to put the brake on, adjust the awning against the sun). It lies with the soles of its feet together, apparently meditating, its diaper beautifully white. Most satisfactory, when I think of the enormous task waiting for me indoors.

Unlike the other place, every room in this house has a clock, though none of them tells the same time. There are also dozens of broken watches lying where they have been dropped. The first thing is to decide (or choose) what time it is, and then synchronise all the clocks. I pick on the kitchen clock, which tells the latest time, twenty-one minutes past nine. Then I realise that if I go from room to room setting all the clocks at twenty-one minutes past nine, it will be at least a quarter to ten by the time I've finished. I can't take the kitchen clock with me, as it is fixed to the wall, so I have to make a different plan. I take the travelling clock from the bedroom (which says four minutes past nine) and adjust the others to that. When I have finished (it was quite a business altering the kitchen clock, standing on a chair and moving the hands forward eleven hours and seventeen minutes, a whirr and a strike on every hour, since I know it's not right to move them backwards) I realise that of course all I had to do was to set the travelling clock at twenty-one minutes past nine and proceed from there. Trust me to do it the hard way. But at least one learns.

Before I can have a bath I have to scrub the rims of

dirt and grease away, all at different levels, and combine the bits of different coloured soap into one multi-coloured tablet. The face flannels are grey and slimy. I daren't throw them away, because I don't know how much money I have to buy new ones, and in any case where would I buy them: I decide to boil them sometime, when I have time, when time permits. When I have put the plastic ducks and boats and deep-sea divers and submarines into a plastic bag, I feel a real sense of achievement. Already the idea of a bath has become a possibility. I rinse a handful of toothbrushes, each one with paste coated on the handles and the bristles. I place them, heads up, in a tumbler (having washed the tumbler first). I have never felt so fired with creativity. This is better, so far, than sitting in my rocking chair, better than journeys and dreams. I lower myself into the hot water and float. The list (only in my mind as yet) becomes interminable, enough to occupy a lifetime. Meanwhile the baby sleeps, the chaos remains untouched except for the bath, the soap, and toothbrushes, the intention of boiling the face flannels.

Bathed, dressed in a shirt and the one pair of jeans I can find that isn't caked with egg or pastry or blood, I confront the problem. But it refuses to be confronted. Where, after all, do I begin? If I start with the shoes—a day's work at least—the kitchen will become uninhabitable. If I start with the kitchen, the mattresses will never get aired, the laundry will never get done. If I do the laundry, when shall I decide what they are going to eat? But then again, how can I cook with all that washing up waiting to be done? One thing is certain: I can't spend another night in this bedroom in the state it's in. I am temporarily baffled, and sit on the bed waiting for inspiration.

The list. Of course I can't begin without the list. I will pin it up somewhere, and refer to it constantly, crossing out each task as it is accomplished. The thing to do is to find a pad of paper and a ballpoint pen, then go from room to room sensibly writing down what has to be done. If only I had some help. God knows where my mother has got to. She would have it done in a jiffy. It really is too bad of them to put me here without my mother. And too bad of my mother to allow it.

Perhaps I could contact her by writing a letter (too slow) or by telephoning: rescue me, help me, what shall I do? Please take me away, take me over, you see I'm only a little girl, I have no real experience. Would she fall for that? She always has; yet somehow I have an awful fear that this time she's not going to. Either my mother has disassociated herself from this plot or enterprise or whatever it is, or she has been cut off. I have to do all this by myself, without help from man or mother. It may take years. I ought to begin.

(And yet why bother? What's the difference? Consider the lilies of the field, how they grow. It'll all come to the same thing in the end, tidy or untidy, clean or dirty. They will grow somehow, even if they have to take devious routes to do it. Whether I become old or not, I will inevitably die. Simply leave the house as it is, and move to another. Start again, with no possessions, a blank slate, an empty glass. I'm too tired already, I'm much too tired.)

Enough of that. Find the pad of paper and the ballpoint pen, that should be easy. Let's have a bit of bustle. I begin to tidy the dressing table, though the washing up nags at my conscience. After a while I find myself wandering about with a handful of five buttons, a number of paper clips, two collar studs, one cleaners' ticket, three postage stamps and a few foreign coins (centimes and lira). I don't know where to put the handful. If I distribute each object in its proper place (wherever that may be) it will take all morning up and down the stairs. I'm tempted to throw the lot away, but that would be shocking: buttons cost money, stamps are valuable, maybe someone will be going to France or Italy soon and will be glad of some small change. At last I compromise by tipping it all into an empty jar, which I place on the mantelpiece. This jar now has a purpose and can be catalogued as Odds & Ends, Jar Of.

I realise now that I haven't had anything to eat since

72

last night's dinner, which I hardly remember. Also the baby is crying. I brutally decide to eat something before attending to the baby, but it is impossible, the creature is becoming frenzied. I take it quite roughly out of its pram, carry it upstairs, change it (throwing the dirty diaper into a corner of the bathroom), feed it, take it downstairs again, dump it in the pram. It is immediately sick, staring at me with accusing eyes. I mop it up with a corner of the sheet, which I then tuck quickly under the mattress again. The baby has been mishandled and resumes its crying, though in a different key. I go upstairs and sit down in the kitchen, blocking my ears. I decide to keep my ears blocked for ten minutes by the clock, which now says twenty-five past two. If the baby is still crying at twenty-five to three I will kill it. What a relief that at twenty-eight minutes to three everything is quiet. I open a tin of beans and eat them cold, with a spoon left over from breakfast. It would have been bizarre to kill the baby. One shouldn't even think of such things.

After the beans, not letting myself rest for a moment (it is getting late, but oh how I long to rest), I start on the washing up. In my mind's eye, which is unreliable, I see a spotless kitchen, everything stowed away orderly, all the cereal tipped into one packet, cheeses covered in muslin, little tarts waiting to be filled, preserves labelled Damson, Ginger, Rhubarb, Apricot, the kettle quietly steaming on a low burner. In fact I merely wash the breakfast and (presumably) supper dishes, wipe them with a damp teacloth and slam them anyhow into cupboards. It will be much better to tidy all the cupboards at once. I will set aside a day for it. Everything will come right in the end.

At least as I sit (finally allowing myself to sit) in the window bay, I can look at the empty draining board, the plate rack propped against the wall, the mop and scourer neat in an empty milk bottle. Fool that I am, I assume that since I have done the washing up, the washing up is done. I could start on the next item on the list, if I had a list. As it is, for just two minutes I sit doing absolutely nothing.

This was impossible before, in the place where there was infinite freedom. I now find that it is a positive act. I sit; my mouth drops open; my eyes glaze; my mind becomes a blank screen, only shuddering now and then with unformed thought. It is the next best thing to being dead; if perfected, it can slip into death with no interruption whatever, not even the flick of an eyelid.

So I am sitting, coasting gently between death and life, when a bombardment startles me. They are coming! They are coming with their satchels bouncing on their backs, their weapons of sport, their ripped sweaters and torn blazers! They are coming, with their ink stains and wounds, new bandages and socks round their ankles! Their mouths are already open, to be crammed with food; they throw their bodies recklessly up the steps, the invaders, the marauders, the victors *ludorum!*

Whatever fear I have known until now seems no more than a little gasp in my sleep, a slight sensation of falling. Now I really know fear. I open my mouth to scream, but no sound comes out. I step forward to find knives, anything to protect myself. They have arrived. My gaping mouth is a smile; my hands, warding them off, welcome them.

9

I'm not sure if I can keep going. I am not sure whether I'm still sane. Mrs. April visits me sometimes. She is kind and worried, rather dismayed by her inability to help me. She inspects the house, approving the small islands of order, noting uncritically the things that still have to be done. She inspects the baby—presumably for sores, bruises and so on—and if any of the children are there, she questions them quietly, seeming satisfied with their answers. Towards the end of her visit, we always have tea, just the two of us, either in the kitchen or the sitting room. She always says the same thing, balancing her cup and saucer on her neat knee:

"Well, do you want to leave?"

"You know I do. But you can see for yourself—there's so much to be done."

"When do you think you'll have it finished?"

"I don't know. Next week, perhaps. Maybe a fortnight."

"Basil Gondzik is asking after you."

"Really?" This conversation becomes a waste of time.

"The weather hasn't been too good again."

"Oh, I'm sorry."

"Well, then, dear. If there's nothing I can do . . ." She

looks round brightly, replaces the cup and saucer on the tray, brushes a crumb from her skirt, "I'll be on my way."

"Thank you for coming." I am allowing myself to be abandoned. Now is the time to cling to her arm, tell her I can't stand it another minute, demand that she take me with her. I show her to the front door. She turns and gives me a little encouraging wave as she goes through the gate. This happens over and over again. I've almost given up hope of a word being changed. If she changed so much as a word I would be horrified.

It's not the hard labour, quite honestly, that's so exhausting: it's the loneliness, the guilt, and the unendurable exercise of loving. I often dream about you now, that you share the bed, that you are walking out of the locked room, that I am waiting for you or that you have just gone away. But when I'm awake, I realise that you are not so much a necessity as a device: someone (or thing) to be used for a purpose. Our love for each other, compared with this marathon I am now engaged in, was, is and will be trivial. Your real life, your most genuine love, is going on far away: so far, that if I could see it all, it would be microscopic, the great noise you make in my dreams dwarfed and inaudible. If you ever think about it (I doubt whether you dream), it is probably the same for you. I have been dead for years, you think, so you have peopled my house with strangers: strangers, that is, to me. And yet I am so alive (except in the moments of doing nothing), so solid, so keenly intent on my tasks, so absorbed, so prone to excitement and intolerable fatigue, so patient and stubborn with this house and its endless chores—how can you imagine me dead? Because I was a device for you, too, and outlived my usefulness. So we threw each other away, along with the bicycles and watches and other expensive machinery that had, through carelessness, stopped functioning. I am not entirely to blame.

One must think about something while (at last) tidying the shoe cupboard; even I can't be entirely concerned with sizes two–five, finding the missing match to the size three wellington boot or the size four dancing slipper. These, roughly, are my thoughts while I play (with shoes) a game called "pelmanism": a frightening game in which two packs of cards are scattered face downwards and the pairing of them depends on memory. I am not entirely to blame for this chaos; to believe that I, alone, created it would be a kind of hubris; to believe that I, alone, must clean it up and restore order (which possibly was never there in the first place) is both arrogant and presumptuous. Even a good gardener can't achieve anything by himself: he must have seeds, plants, tools, a patch of fertile ground. Like Oedipus, I have never broken the law, for the simple reason that I have never been conscious of doing so. Why, then, blind myself? Why this continual *mea culpa*? Why the self-disgust? Why this smug conviction that every misfortune is a punishment, every weakness an original sin? In fact I don't know the answers to these questions, or indeed whether there are answers. But at least I ask them. That must be something.

The shoe cupboard is finished, all the shoes arranged in sizes, the odd ones thrown away (unable to convince myself that I may sometime have a one-legged child); the baby grows: I have mended a lot of ragged clothes and found a kind of satisfaction in shirt buttons and pyjama cords; I cook, we eat, I wash the dishes; I am getting quite good at finding lost property and returning it to its rightful owner; they have come to think of me as judge, provider, oracle, scullery maid, scapegoat, a begrudged necessity and a reliable irritant. My fear is usually controlled, I can assume the insouciance of a lion tamer or a snake charmer when it threatens. On the surface there is a haphazard attempt at order, but every cupboard except one is still bulging with rubbish, every drawer is a confusion of knives and cotton reels and spoons and string and skewers and the tops of paste pots. In order to survive (I hope) with some sort of sanity, I've learned to adapt myself to the chaos until such time (if ever) I can control it. I know that the thread is in with the teaspoons, the carving knife on top of the piano, the sock on the fourth row of books on the left of the fireplace, the buttons in the Odds & Ends, Jar Of. In this way, of course, I am making quite sure that I'm indispensable, for how could anyone else manage?

"Well, do you want to leave?"

"You know I do. But you can see for yourself—there's so much to be done."

"When do you think you'll have it finished?"

"I don't know. Next week, perhaps. Maybe a fortnight."

Mistakenly, perhaps, I don't tell Mrs. April my private thoughts about not being solely responsible, my suspicions that I am in fact innocent. She might take me away if she thought I wasn't expiating my guilt. So I begin to tidy by day and make havoc by night, in the attempt to make time stand still. As a result of this cunning notion, the level of disorder appears to remain the same, or at the most only slightly lower. I am heartily glad that I never made the list, for it would have revealed my dishonesty. There is another look in Mrs. April's mild eye: it could be suspicion, but I prefer to believe it's bewilderment. We still don't alter a word of our conversation. Gondzik is always asking after me, the weather is never very good. I firmly believe that this state of affairs will last forever, provided I don't make any active move to change it.

* * *

The baby is growing older. That's nice. He walks and speaks and runs; he reads and writes and draws pictures of amphibious cars. He is moody—affectionate, aggressive, cheerful, withdrawn, thoughtful, sullen. He goes away from the house now, and although of course I keep busy (mostly with preparations for his return) my heart is suspended during his absence; you could say I'm absent-hearted, not really listening to anything except for the sound of his heavy feet on the steps, not really seeing anything until he comes, talking vaguely (to myself or to

Mrs. April) until I can talk to him again, though heaven knows everything I say to him is pretty banal. I have been proud of each height he has attained—three feet, four feet eight, five feet six, and now he is taller than I am. It is an unequal relationship in that I believe him to be perfect, whereas he knows (and frequently exaggerates) my imperfections. Also, of course, he knows other people, and I only know him, the children and Mrs. April. Never mind all that. We manage.

The children have taken to staying away for longer and longer periods; in fact I'm not at all sure when I last saw them. This makes it much more difficult to keep the place untidy, but between us we do our best. The nursery floor, for instance, is still thick with broken toys, though no one has been there since the beginning of time.

"Well, do you want to leave?" Mrs. April asks patiently.

"You know I do. But you can see for yourself—there's so much to be done."

"When do you think you'll have it finished?"

"I don't know. Next week, perhaps. Maybe a fortnight."

As I now have, in fact, very little to do—disarranging takes no time at all—I have far less opportunity for thought. Thought has nothing to latch on to. My good moments of doing nothing are also disturbed: I am always in a state of waiting. I wait all day every day, and most of the nights. The person who was the baby doesn't come back for tea, for supper; he is not there at breakfast. He is not there at all. I search the house for him. I will clean it, tidy it, turn out all the cupboards and drawers, fill it with flowers and music and chocolate if only he will come back. He will surely arrive tomorrow.

Mrs. April turns up with her colleague.

"We have come to take you back, dear."

"Oh, no. You see I am waiting."

"There's no point in waiting."

"But you can see for yourself—there's so much to be done."

"There's nothing you can do. There's no more to be done."

"But supposing he comes and there's no one here?"

"He won't come. Basil Gondzik is asking after you. The weather hasn't been too good again."

With great kindness, handling me very gently, they take my arms and carry me back across the lawn, my feet hardly brushing the grass. It is early morning. The lily pond, the trees, the house itself emerging out of a thick mist. My windows are still open. The deck chairs on the terrace are soggy with dew or rain. When they get me to my room they put me to bed; I sleep for a long time, without dreaming.

PART
THREE

10

I now believe that the purpose of this place is to repeat experience until it is remembered: a gross over-simplification, no doubt. Gondzik is very interested in my stay abroad. He questions me incessantly about the smallest detail. But although I can recount it accurately enough, I can't re-create it. He will never know what it was really like. I can show him my scarred hands, but can only describe to him (stammering, uncertain, inarticulate) the state of my heart. But a fulfilled heart, surely, he asks; a colossal human achievement? What rubbish. Sitting in my rocking chair I still find myself watching for the person (who was the baby) to come strolling out from the trees, arm round a girl's neck as though to strangle her; they tussle and chase each other in circles, then rest, legs dangling, on the wall round the lily pond. But I am frightened of actually seeing them. In my imagination I can make them accessible.

The cast has altered slightly, Elizabeth gone (though Gondzik says only temporarily), Hermann gone, Rowena changed her appearance, Revlon abdicated in favour of Dominic, Simon and George established. Mavis welcomes me back warmly, with a whole babble of stories which I understand better—or at least differently—than I did before. There is a new girl, Leonora, who laughs like a hyena, without mirth. She is by no means unattractive (the blonde, I hear, was very caustic when she arrived), but out of her rather stony little face breaks this awful laughter which makes our blood run cold. She has a habit of marching up to people and saying imperiously, "I want to talk to you. Now." But then she has nothing to say. She simply laughs in your face and struts away, insulted.

I thought at least the office situation would be resolved, but it isn't. All sorts of predictions float around as to when the Director will resign; whether he'll resign; whether he'll be sued for mismanagement or whether, in fact, he may have already committed suicide and is operating through a set of mirrors. I have lost whatever interest I had in the case. I forget to pass on rumours. As far as politics are concerned, even Gondzik learns to leave me alone.

I have other concerns which begin, very soon after my return, with the dog. Just as I predicted or remembered, she comes racing towards me on the pool path, ears back, coat streaming, ruddered by a plumed tail. Wildly barking, she flings herself at me head-on, practically knocking me over; she circles me in a frenzy then suddenly cringes, grovelling, dragging herself round on her stomach, going through every servile trick to make me feel badly. All right, I'll take you over. Now she leaps more like a lamb than a dog, all feet together, springing through the wood alongside me but keeping a wary eye on my possible treachery. When we reach the pool she lies down, behaving correctly, in a patch of shade, her whole body heaving with the heat and the exertion.

Owning a dog, my routine begins to change. I feel guilty about the dog, which must have fields, ditches, rabbits, bracken, a variety of smells. Also I am more confident in her presence. I venture paths where I have never been before. I see no one as yet, but very often the dog stiffens, alerts, barks at shadows. At night she creeps under my bed; if I wake and call her (thinking she's gone), her tail thuds between bed and floor like a heartbeat.

Gondzik has two entirely opposed views about the dog. On the one hand, he thinks she takes me out of myself (which is apparently desirable); on the other, he thinks that I arranged for her to come just when she did, and that I am using her as a substitute for the people who have left me. This is not desirable. In vain I try to convince him that the dog is a dog, and a very inadequate substitute for anything but a dog. Even while he strides along with her, barking meaningless commands, he is fathoming deep meanings to this dog. I was put through the ordeal of the house, he says, in order to experience desolation. What am I doing, trying to cheat desolation with a dog? And so on. I have got to the stage now when I let him think what he likes. So long as he is with me I am as protected as being with an irritating nursemaid. I think about something else, usually going over the house in my mind and deciding what I would have done there, had there been time.

Gondzik now decides—quite arbitrarily, it seems to me—that I am a woman. He no longer touches me. He has given up scrabbling in my mouth, probably feeling it to be incestuous, and has become (according to his lights) properly parental. This is a terrible pass for my Zotkind to come to; he knew (without consciously knowing) that a successful lover is parent, sibling, child, not to mention the minor gods. Gondzik is strictly compartmentalised. I am a woman: therefore I am unhealthy without a man (and particularly unhealthy with a dog). I must find one, there are plenty about. I answer flippantly enough that when a woman devised these things, she created only the Father, the Son and the Holy Spirit. Then what is my Holy Spirit, Gondzik asks earnestly. He is like a doctor trying to determine whether I'm getting sufficient vitamins. As usual, I can't think of a sensible answer, so don't answer at all.

Nevertheless, as the attack goes on, gathers momentum (starting as subtle asides, becoming ever more explicit and enraged), I begin to feel dreadfully inadequate. It's true that after that time of activity (however great the suppressed fear) I am terribly lonely. If they were going to put me in that house, with all those things to be done and all those people to love, they might at least have the charity to let me forget it. As it is, Gondzik plays on my longing for physical contact until the very air surrounding me seems hostile. Perhaps Gondzik is right. I would like to smile more easily. It is not enough that the dog makes me smile. As in the period before the entertainment, I see myself to be old and ugly, but now I react to it with despair and venom (exactly as Gondzik has planned?). The dog, possibly feeling her insufficiency, looks as though she is about to be hanged.

If I could hit back at Gondzik by becoming actively sexual and political, I would feel exonerated. But as I've already discovered, I'm a hopeless audience and I can't act. Gondzik creates a non-stop entertainment in his head, at which he observes himself raping, buggering, being eaten and digested by a multi-racial confederacy of girls. This fantasy seems to him quite satisfactory. He is fortunate. The other, whom I once knew (or will, pray god, know eventually) only cared for the long slow thrust, the crescendo of mutual pleasure that could culminate, at last, in the rite of conception. Childish, perhaps. Dull. A dull child, I stubbornly continue to believe that the most potent aphrodisiac is love.

(I dreamed that you were driving at night, in Africa, with a girl whom you had picked up in a bar. It was very dark, with a warm wind. There was some obstacle in the road, a gate, a level crossing. The girl got out of the car to deal with it. As she stood in the road, erect, mysterious, you turned to me and told me that you were feeling the greatest sexual desire of your life. I understood you completely. This disproved my belief but was, as far as I was concerned, only a dream.)

I don't tell Gondzik any of this, he would scoff. I begin to feel that I shouldn't spend so much time with him, that he is destructive to me. But when there is so much time, spending it becomes irrelevant; it's necessary to give it away in great armfuls when loneliness threatens. This is the poor reason for allowing Gondzik to criticise whatever I say or do or am or have been. As for what will be, unless I can find a relationship of which he approves he tries (successfully) to make me believe I'm beyond hope or help. Turning my confidences against me, he now states that what he once called a colossal human achievement was no more than an arid mistake. Why did I stay away so long? Out of cowardice, he says, before I can answer. I am self-loving, self-absorbed, self-obsessed; why can't I beg, like any other woman; why can't I admit that the greatest achievement of all is to be humble with men (and Gondzik)? Pleasure begins, he says (throwing a stick for the dog), where morality ends.

I don't understand what morality has got to do with it. Perhaps in Gondzik's view, the Director and his staff are having fun: it is commonly agreed that they have left morality behind and are flouting the accepted rules of decency and virtue. Gondzik, too, is ardently concerned with flouting these rules; yet in him, it seems, this is commendable. The fact is that he can't do without morality: without that spur he would have no pleasure, he wouldn't be able to indulge himself in evil, he wouldn't be able to congratulate himself on being a law-breaker. Whereas I, long since cast off from morality, a believer solely in convenience, am becalmed, no wind to fill my sails.

I don't know how long my life will be, whether it will be spent here, whether they will take me to another part of the place or whether I shall return where I came from. But here and now, whether I die this evening or not, Gondzik has convinced me that life is insufferable. Something must be done. I must capture that elusive energy that got me out of bed in the mornings at the house. Someone or something must make demands on me. I try to pick up rumours again, but Dominic says the staff are all on holiday, nothing doing in the office. So I confront (furtively) the men, trying to pick one who will, in Gondzik's eyes, be good for me.

The trouble is that my eyes are not only a different colour from Gondzik's, they are a different sex. If I had male eyes I could inspect the available flesh with casual good humour, discussing it with my friends. I go to the pool, scanning the men from behind dark glasses. They would be horrified if they knew what I was up to, these fellatio addicts, these consumers of *Playboy* and *Penthouse* whose hatred of women so far surpasses mine of them. I try to find promise in white blubber, sloping shoulders, flat feet, monstrous growths of body hair or chests as pallid and enfeebled as a breastless woman. One walks with thighs pressed together, buttocks clenched, as though in agony to relieve himself; another swings along like an ape, knuckles, brushing the ground. It is impossible to find out whether any of them are loveable (which, according to my belief, should make them appetising), for they seem to inhabit a world in which love has never existed. They are pleasant enough, to be sure, nodding to each other, making civil gestures; once in the water, they even communicate by means of splashing, shouting, throwing a ball about, roaring a good deal. But if they were women they would make themselves sick; they would laugh at themselves and tell cruel jokes in the locker room. I, being far too ambitious, am looking for someone with the body of a boy, the wisdom of a father, the sensibility of a woman and the strength of Almighty God.

Rebelliously obedient to Gondzik, I turn to the men who stay indoors. Some of them are homosexuals, at least two of them very beautiful. But I can't set out to conquer alien ground. They form a small group, really easy only in each other's company. The habits of minorities die hard, and even the most emancipated of them seems on the look-out for persecution. "Queer as a coot" joins "working like a black" and "Jew-boy" as a term of abuse. "Just like a woman" is also, to say the least, in bad taste. The rules of communication became more and more stringent. I merely (for a start) want to hold someone's hand.

The only man for whom I feel the slightest attraction (in the male sense) is Simon, who looks like a gloomy adolescent and talks with the wit of a middle-aged don. Maybe it would work splendidly on a desert island; here (although we're supposed to be timeless), the disparity in our ages makes any kind of approach unthinkable. He may be much older than I, but whichever way you look at it we couldn't even loosely, even by a decade or two, be called contemporaries. I am not to blame for these ancient laws, remember, and cannot consciously break them. This only leaves George, so George (to try and put up some sort of a show for Gondzik) it must be.

Gondzik, conniving, provides me with drink. The dog, conniving, takes a fancy to George. We go for walks, and see nothing extraordinary. I even find the vegetable garden again, prolific as before, but empty. George is what I suppose to be a normal man. Of average height and weight and age, he would make (or has made) a good husband, soldier or civil servant. I continually forget what he looks like, and try to imprint on my mind his average face: without success, for the moment he is out of sight it's gone again. I realise that the reason I cannot know George is that I have never known him before. That's why I can't recognise him. We are complete strangers to each other.

At this point I want to give up, the enterprise seems quite hopeless. But Gondzik goads me on. Search, he says, ferret out, pursue, investigate, pry if necessary; there has got to be something recognisable in George, something that will touch or move me. Find out what his political views are, for a start. I do. They are average. He must have brought something with him, some experience he can't yet remember. I try, and find a perfectly clear recollection of an average family, wife and two children, nothing hidden away. Gondzik says this is impossible, I'm not making enough effort: make him lose his head, Gondzik insists, sweep him off his feet. Me? Yes, you! But how do I do that, how set about it? Blind him with money and fame? Buy him outright? Send him flowers every day? Or (reversing sexes) strip, coo, purr, yelp a little? You're hopeless, Gondzik says, slamming his chapel door.

It's true. I am. And the curious thing is that as soon as I become hopeless, George begins to reveal himself a little. I find that his face, in certain lights and at certain times, is wry. He has a higher than average knowledge of golf and Glen Miller. He is very slightly puzzled about his mother and grandmother, tending to confuse them with each other. He doesn't know why he is here, but imagines it's something to do with an old war wound which troubles him occasionally. He even hints, with average slyness, at average love affairs he has had while away from home. He kisses me good night with average passion.

Gondzik is enchanted. He says I look better already. Lord, but he's a fool. And yet if I allow myself to think Gondzik a fool I shall no longer have any guidance or anchor at all in this place. I must go on in the belief that he is right. There's no alternative. Finally, coldly, making the required sounds and gestures, I seduce George. He keeps his underpants on. It is such an average experience that it can't be justified or regretted, praised or condemned, remembered or forgotten. However, when I wake the next morning I am at least able to think that I have made a life, of sorts.

* * *

At breakfast next morning Gondzik marches in like a man with something weighty on his mind. But where, as the artificial orange juice, the coffee and the eggs take their dread course, is George? He didn't sleep with me, of course. Has he overslept? Is he ill or angry? What was before a merely average presence becomes, suddenly, a very positive absence. My life (of sorts)? Where is my average life? I worked for it, where has it gone?

Nobody mentions George. I run to find Mavis. No, dear,

I don't know at all. I run to George's room, along dozens of corridors. Locked. No answer to my knocking. I run back, upstairs, downstairs, upstairs again to Gondzik's virginal eyrie.

"Where's George?"

He smiles with pretty teeth and lips, eyes gentle. "George? He's gone."

I throw myself on him, hammering with clenched fists. He nods slowly, smiling, as though congratulating me.

11

The entertainers have gone, the air is a little sharper. Realising now that all they intend to do here is cheat me, I decide to escape. I am not going to confide in Gondzik, who told me I could leave without difficulty at any time. He is not to be trusted, I'm sure he's in league with whoever it is who wants to trap me. I must therefore make plans of my own. The first thing is to try and find out the lie of the land and which direction I should take.

The dog, of course, always comes with me on my explorations: her senses are much sharper than mine. I make an arbitrary choice of north, south, east and west, deciding that the statue in the lily pond faces north. Guided by this, I make a rough map of the places I know: the mansion, the pool, the vegetable garden. I can't put the house in, because I have no idea where it is. I also draw a rough circle for the lake, where Gondzik saw the skater.

Every day after breakfast, when I am dressed, the dog and I set out, each day going a little farther, each day adding something to the map. We put in a tower in the woods (apparently uninhabited), various glades with statues and rustic seats, a couple of full-size houses (shuttered and locked) and, at last, the office. This too is closed for the holiday, but it is obviously the office as it is a modern building with a tarmac driveway which is noticed No Entry, No Parking, No Loading or Unloading, Trespassers Will be Prosecuted, No Dogs, No Bare Feet and Forbidden to Spit. I am very tempted to take my sandals off and enter with the dog, spitting; but since there is obviously no one there, it would be pointless. However, it is helpful to have it on my map, and if things get really desperate I now intend to burgle it at night. Curiously enough, it doesn't seem to be guarded, and the holiday might be a good time to try.

One day we find a very old woman sitting in a garden chair under the pines, a tea tray by her side on a small table. The dog, of course, approaches her first, tail wagging, nose inquisitive. I lurk about among the trees for a while, until I see that the old woman is glad to meet the dog, and is indeed offering her a piece of broken biscuit.

"Well, well, doggy," the old woman says aloud, "and where do you come from?"

I walk over the soft pine needles on moccasined feet. Seeing me, the old woman tries to rise from her chair. I say "Don't get up" and, since her face seems to be lifted expectantly, kiss her papery cheek. There are two cups on the tray, a tea cosy on the teapot. She settles back, apparently ready for some sort of diversion, her hands folded in her lap. Sitting on the ground, I pour the tea into shallow china cups, she takes hers with a trembling hand, so I make room for it on the tray. I'm so suspicious now that I think the old woman may be someone else in disguise, a bait to lure me into talking. Hugging my knees, I ask, "Tell me a story.'

"A story?" The little face puffs into incredulous self-ridicule. "I've forgotten all my stories."

"No, you haven't. Go on. Once upon a time . . ."

"Well." She thinks for a moment, head cocked, hazel eye fastening on a high branch. The dog cocks her head also, looking up. "Well, once upon a time . . ."

"Long ago?"

"Long ago. There was a little girl who wished she was

a pirate or a Red Indian or a giant in seven-league boots. Most little girls want to be princesses and fairies and . . . well, pretty things of that sort. But this little girl whose name was Dora—"

"*Dora?*"

"Yes. Dora. This little girl was going to fight Mudjekee-wis with the fatal Wawbeek—"

"The what?"

"She loved the tales of the Norsemen, all about Thor and Odin and Loke and Balder the Beautiful who was killed, you know, by a dart of mistletoe thrown by his brother Hoder, who was blind. Of course he didn't mean to do it. Yes, Dora was very stubborn, a bit of a hobbledehoy really . . ." The old woman drifts off for a moment. I wait for her to continue. So far the story is not very interesting. "And her main fault was, *she believed every-thing she was told!*" Dramatic pause. I think rapidly. "There was a lady in the village—the schoolmaster's wife, as it happens—who was going to have a baby, and she told Dora that when it came she would sell it to Dora for six-pence. Now Dora's parents weren't rich and they gave her a penny a week to buy peppermints and so on. There was only one shop in the village and this was run by an old crone called Mrs. Jessup, a nice old thing but she was doubled up with arthritis and Dora was perfectly con-vinced she was a witch. Anyway. For six long weeks Dora saved up her pennies and on the day when she was given her sixth penny—it was a Saturday—she set off down the road with the six copper pennies in her hand, striding along pretending she was a giant. She went in through the schoolmaster's gate and knocked on the schoolmaster's door, and in a few minutes the schoolmaster's wife came to the door—"Hullo, Dora, have you come to see the baby?" The old woman is an excellent mimic, and is now well into her stride. "No," said Dora, and held out the six pennies, "I've come to buy it." Oh, how the schoolmaster's wife laughed! "Well, did you ever, imagine Dora thinking she could buy a baby for sixpence!" her face crumples.

I am not amused. "So what happened then?"

"Dora went into a terrible tantrum, she was inconsolable. And she decided that whatever else she did, however many battles she fought (and won, of course) and however many prisoners she got out of prison and however famous she became as a poet or however great she became as a king, she would *revenge herself* on that schoolmaster's poor wife!"

"So what did she do?"

"She grew up and had a great many babies and grew old and died," the old woman says simply, with a final air.

I am appalled. The air in the woods seems ice cold. I have gooseflesh on my arms and legs. The old woman levers herself up, finds a shawl which she efficiently wraps round her shoulders, a stick which she grasps firmly in her right hand and totters off through the trees. I call "Goodbye!" but she doesn't hear me. I want to follow her, but she is out of sight. Have mercy, be merciful. Our Father, who art in heaven, Hallowed by thy Name. Thy kingdom come. Thy will be done, On earth as it is in heaven. Give us this day our daily bread. And forgive us our trespasses, As we forgive those who trespass against us. And lead us not into temptation. . . . For thine is the kingdom, the power, and the glory, for ever and ever. Amen. Having prayed as well as I can remember, I try to hold the dog for comfort but she squirms away and is off through the trees in the direction of what she knows as home.

Can this be all there is to a life? Are those really the bare bones of it? Nothing else? No loom, no spinning wheel: nothing? What about love and thought, acts of creation and acts of madness? Must eyes have drawn blinds forever, hearts lock their doors? Is it all just a cruel prank played by the ignorant on the innocent (by you on me, who could never see the joke)? For God's sake (who also delivers us from evil) get me out of this playground, let me see the world as a whole, let me know where I am and what I can hope for, expect or dread.

I stumble back to the house, find the dog waiting patiently at the back door. For a while, some days I suppose, I stay in my room, pleading minor illness. Gondzik takes the dog out and, rather surprisingly, brings me food. I keep the blinds down and walk long distances between the furniture, I sit in the chairs, lie on the bed, pounding and pummelling my empty head until it hums, but reveals nothing. Sometimes I look at my map, but the immensity of what isn't there defeats me. I passionately envy the dead, who have no future. Death smiles, but I don't know how to reach it, the usual methods are unavailable and I have little ingenuity.

"There is an old woman," I say to Gondzik one day. "She must live in the woods. Bring her here. I want her."

Gondzik considers. "I don't know any old woman."

"Then ask. Someone must know her."

He says he has asked, and that no one knows her.

"Why don't you go out and find her yourself?"

"I can't. I'm ill."

"Mrs. April could go with you."

"No, no, no!" My fists clench, I'm beside myself with fear. "I don't want to see Mrs. April! I don't ever want to see her again!"

"Very well." The door closes; I'm alone again.

One day I pull up the blind a few inches. Some of the trees are growing rusty; a pheasant stands so still on the grass that I think it's pottery. There is a faint smell of burning, and the insects have been washed off my netting by the rain. The map, with its immense deserts, lies on the table. The dog (who must have forgotten that there was once light in this room) runs at me and knocks with her front paws, uttering small demanding barks. It's such a long time since I went to the pool. Do leaves float in it now? Does Gondzik still battle about in the water? Is it warm? When do they empty the pool? Will it soon be winter? The dog scratches at my leg as though it were a door. I put on my swimsuit and smock, find my dreary towel, pack my chattels, steal out of my room, uselessly telling the dog to be quiet. She leaps down the red-carpeted stairs, stopping on each landing to make sure I am still there.

I remember that the way to the pool is very straightforward, but again I lose my way, finding myself in a sunny orchard with russet apples festooning the trees. They aren't ripe yet, but some of them have already fallen. I throw them for the dog, who is crazed with happiness bringing each one back in her slavering jaws, then refusing to be parted from it. There is a large wooden hut in the orchard, with smoke creeping out of a rusty chimney. I approach it cautiously but with determination, in case the old woman is inside with her kettle. The windows are clean, and there is indeed furniture, somebody lives there, somebody is sitting in an armchair. I push the door, with one finger, a mere inch; but the foolish dog bounds against it and rushes in with all the pandemonium of a dog unexpectedly returned from a long journey. The gardener peers round the wing of his armchair, amazed by this visitation.

What am I to do? I step backwards towards the sun. "Come in, come in," he snaps impatiently.

"I was just . . ."

"And close the door behind you, it makes the stove smoke."

He is just as I remembered, except that today he wears a tie and a greenish pullover. I sit down well out of reach, measuring the distance to the closed door. The dog collapses in front of the stove with a huge sigh of relief.

"Well, how are you today?"

"All right." I'm very wary.

"You must never be unhappy."

"I've been very unhappy."

"Why?"

"I can't stand it in that place. I'm imprisoned. I don't

97

know what's going to happen tomorrow. I'm lonely. I don't see any point in living."

"You shouldn't be in that place," he says firmly, lighting his pipe with three matches. "It's no place for you. You should be free. I don't know why they took you there, it must have been a mistake."

"You really think so?"

He nods energetically, puffing. "Freedom to live, that's what you need. Break through these petty restrictions. You're an artist, a free spirit. You were born to be beautiful and to create beauty. They don't understand."

"They don't understand."

"But I understand."

"Yes, you understand."

"Remember I'm always here.'"

"You'll give me sanctuary?"

"Of course. Anytime."

"You mean . . . you really believe I have a life worth living?"

"Life! What can you do with life but live it? Live it to the utmost! Live it to the full! Why let them clip your wings? You should soar, soar . . ." He makes a vague and expansive gesture towards the smoky ceiling. "Life is a great and glorious experience, it can't survive behind bars. Break away, my darling, break loose, break out! I don't know a single intelligent person, but for you, out there"—again he encompasses the universe—"there are riches, gems, diamonds of wisdom and love!"

I am deeply impressed, but one thing still troubles me. I ask, "Do you know the old woman who has tea in the woods?"

"Marriage is the coffin of love! Remember that. Sex is a great and glorious experience, it can't survive behind bars." He seems to be growing a little tired. "Anytime you need me . . ."

"I've been planning to escape."

"Excellent, excellent. And so you should."

"Can I come here?"

"I'm always here, anytime you need me. Mustn't lose hope, mustn't be trapped." He seems to be falling asleep, so I get up quietly.

"Thank you. Thank you very much. I hope I can find the way."

"Dog'll show you," he mumbles. The pipe has fallen onto his chest, where it is burning a black hole in his pullover. I take it gently and put it in an ashtray, then tiptoe out, shooing the dog in front of me, and close the door.

What an incredible piece of luck. No don't think of it like that. What a clarion message from the future. What hope, what security. Supposing he does ask something in return—well I'll give it gladly, since I'm so indebted. At last I have purpose, an identity. I'm not going to live my life in one sentence. I'm going to fight great battles, rescue prisoners from prison, score the sky with my poetry, rule as a benevolent and mighty king. I run with the dog stripping small pieces of bark from the apple trees so that I will be able to find my way back if the dog forgets. In the orchard I find a stick and make a trail in the sandy path putting heaps of sticks and pine cones at each intersection. At last I see the mansion (to my left, when I thought it would be to my right). It seems to be evening, since lights are on. If I am late for dinner, I must think of a satisfactory explanation for Gondzik, and carelessly ask him, perhaps, when he thinks it will next be full moon.

12

I don't, in fact, ask Gondzik (he is too wily), but work out
for myself that it will be about twenty-one nights until the
moon is full. As I have no flashlight or matches (Mavis
would get me matches, but again I'm too cautious to ask
her), a full moon will be necessary if I'm to find my way
back to the gardener's hut by night.

Strange things happen while I'm waiting. I'm haunted,
not by ghosts, but by men. The first one comes through the
locked door behind the screen, letting himself in as easily
as though it were his own room. I am in bed, and he sits
down in the rocking chair, smiling at me, rocking back and
forth. He is elegant, though rather dishevelled. He looks
over my life a little, writing down salient points in a
small notebook, very gentle and attentive. Then he kisses
me good night with a long, thoughtful, exploratory kiss. I
lie back, but he leaves with his notebook, going through the
same door. After a time of frustration and longing I get up
and try to open the door. It is immovable. I never see him
again.

The next one appears in a belvedere in the gardens,
which I am carefully adding to the map. He too is elegant,
but beautifully dressed. Leaning forward, elbows on the
creases of his knees, he takes my hand, gazing meaning-

fully into my eyes, speaking in the soft, beautifully modulated tones of an actor. Naturally, I fall in love. He strokes the back of my head, folds me in his arms, I slip into him (I feel) forever. Then he gets up and walks easily away, taking with him shoulders, hips, hands and mouth. I never see him again either, though sometimes he intrudes on my dreams.

After this, they search me out every day. I can see them coming through the woods or along the path, but it's some time before I learn to run in the opposite direction, the dog barking at my heels. To begin with the sweetness of the conversation and the kiss is too alluring. They promise me the pleasure of eternal peace, or the peace of eternal pleasure. Their mouths are soft, their bodies graceful, they carry their entire lives in the inside pockets of their jackets, above the heart. They allow me to believe that they will stay, and that I needn't escape after all. They don't make me believe it, of course. To them I am simply a woman they meet and comfort, kissing me better before they continue on their way. They aren't responsible. It takes many such meetings before I can convince myself of this, and then the slightest shadow on the horizon and I am gone, racing back to the pool or the mansion where everyone except the untouchables is ugly and raucous and trivial, thank God. I barricade all my doors, moving three of my four dressing tables against them. By the time the moon is full, my sexual turmoil has become intolerable, I am tormented with greed, the torture (at least) has been entirely satisfactory.

So that by the time the night comes, the idea of escaping from the place has been almost surplanted by the idea of escaping to the gardener. Old and heavy and outrageous he may be, but he believes in my freedom and he is full of lechery made even more powerful by shame. He will be responsible for me, and has already promised his protection. The torture of the beautiful men has in some way convinced me that the gardener is inevitable in the end;

that my original meeting with him is the only solace I can remember.

There are very few preparations, I have nothing to take except the dog. In order to keep her quiet, I tie a handkerchief round her jaws, talking to her gently meanwhile and stroking her, even smiling at the ridiculous sight she presents with her bandage on. We wait and wait, long after everything is quiet. Holding the dog by her loose scruff (she has no lead or collar) I cautiously open the one unobstructed door. As usual, a few lamps are still on. The moonlight floods through the great stained-glass window on the stairway and one by one, pulling their slender chains, I turn out the lamps in case, as I suspect, they are bugging devices. I have the map under my arm. Bending to hold the somewhat bewildered dog, I creep down the stairs by the red, blue, turquoise and golden light of the window. The indoor fountain drips so loudly and monotonously that it will cover the sound of my barefoot steps. The door leading out to the terrace is difficult; it is very heavy, and in order to slide it back I have to leave go of the dog, but the good creature sits understandingly until I have the door sufficiently open to edge through it.

Terrace, deck chairs, lawn, trees, woods are deep in moonlight. I look up at the mansion. Every window is dark. I let the dog free, but don't untie the handkerchief until we are out of earshot. Silent as swift shadows, we run across the grass into the concealing trees.

Now, beginning to feel frightened, I have to find the orchard. After all this time my heaps of sticks and pine cones have been scattered. But the dog trots confidently ahead, taking the left path, then the right. I decide to trust the dog rather than my unreliable map. From time to time she stops, one front paw lifted, looking back for me. At last I see the clearing, the orchard grass, the marked apple trees. The dog barks once, expecting me to throw apples, I suppose. To keep her quiet I throw one, she bounds off into the shadows. My heartbeat deafens me, my hands are sweating, my legs feel heavy. I plod on until I see a light in the window of the gardener's hut, and the dog, lying camouflaged in grass, gets up to lead me to the door.

Now the knowledge of the welcome, the embrace, the celebration in that hut is almost too much for me. Can I endure it? To be home at last is incredible; but now, finally, I can believe the incredible. I touch the wooden wall of the hut, tacky with tar; the rusty drainpipe; I puncture with my fingernail a blister on the green paint of the door. I am familiar here. I can do what I like. I even have a fancy that the old woman may be somewhere inside, sleeping by her tea tray. I haven't prepared an explanation, because I know none is needed. I knock gently on the door.

After a few moments he opens it, peering out. I am smiling, ready to step inside. The dog, not caring for such subtleties, has gone in already. He sees me at last and says, rather inappropriately I think, "My God!"

"I'm here."

He steps back, and I enter. In determined gratitude, I put my arms round his neck and pull his bulk towards me. He unlatches my arms as though they were a collar. Carelessly (after all, there is all the time in the world) I go into the room. The stove has burned low, he must put more coal on. The dog is already lying in front of it, quite at home. I turn, feeling so light with relief and happiness that I am almost floating.

"I escaped. I'm sorry I was so long, but I had to wait for the moon so that I could see. It was quite easy."

"What are you doing here, why have you come, what are you talking about?"

I laugh. The poor old gardener, he's quite dismayed. I'll make him a cup of cocoa, take care of him. "Why don't you sit down? I'll tell you about it."

Now I have to seduce him. This wasn't in my plan, but shouldn't be difficult. He sits obediently, and I sit at his knee, my elbows on his knees, smiling up at him. His stubby hands, which explored me with such eagerness, hang quite empty on either side of the chair.

"I did what you told me, I broke out and I broke away, I came to you to be free because I was so unhappy, I don't mind about the riches and diamonds and all that, but I would like to be free here in the orchard, and if you like I will stay forever."

He is like someone on whose face the wind has changed: petrified. His eyes stare open, his mouth gapes, his rigid nose has stopped breathing. I kiss him gently, the kiss of life, he is galvanised.

"Who saw you come?"

"No one."

"Did you tell anyone you were coming?"

"Of course not."

"Does anyone know you have been here before?"

"No."

He erupts from the chair, I fall against the iron fender.

"Preposterous!" He charges across the room and back again, standing over me. "Preposterous!"

Either I have been momentarily stunned, or I'm seeing visions: I see two yellow butterflies dancing together in the sunlight, catch-as-catch-can in the summer air. "But you said . . ."

"What do you think my job here is worth? Nothing? I work all day, I dig and hoe and rake and use the best natural fertilisers! I am paid a good salary, do you hear, a good salary! I have this excellent hut rent free, they give me a coal allowance for my heating and my hot-water system! I have worked my way up to head gardener, my tomatoes are the best in the country, my marrow squash win valuable prizes! And you jeopardise all this by creeping in here like a thief in the night! Preposterous!" Suddenly calming, he focuses on me lying with my head against the fender. "You are quite mad," he says, with absolute authority.

"But you took me into the greenhouse. . . ." I haven't the strength to go on, and in any case he is rummaging on the other side of the room. He comes back with a hank of thin rope and a knife. Breathing heavily now, he cuts a length of rope, slams my legs together and binds my ankles. Turning me like a carcass, he pulls my arms behind me and binds my wrists. I don't cry for help. I don't try to resist him. He scoops me up and throws me face downwards over his shoulder. The blood runs to my head, I am blacking out. I hear my voice calling "Old woman! Old woman! Where are you?" Then I hear a door slam and am bumping through the darkness, hearing his rasping breathing as he runs.

When I become conscious again, I am heaped on the terrace. There are blinding lights, the searchlights I knew about. Squinting up, I see that everyone is there: Gondzik, Dominic, Rowena, Simon, Revlon, the interrupted blonde, all in a state of sleepy dishevellment. There is also someone else, a man in pyjamas and a silk dressing gown. I can tell from his bare feet, only a few inches from my face, that he has been hurriedly summoned.

"I brought her straight back, sir," the gardener is saying, his voice sweet with humility. "I thought that was the right thing to do, sir. I thought you would deal with her, sir, as you think fit. I'm only a gardener, sir, and I know my place."

I scream, "Where is the dog? *Where is the dog?*"

"What dog?" the Director asks. "What is she talking about?"

"She had a dog, sir, a mangy sort of mongrel. It should be put down, if you ask me."

"Can you see to that?"

"Certainly, sir. I shall see that it's humane."

"Very good. Gondzik, will you take her to the West Wing?"

I am gathered up again, though this time in Gondzik's arms. Cradling me, he carries me a long distance.

PART
FOUR

13

After a while, seeing the whiteness all around me, I thought I was in Gondzik's room. I remembered that he had carried me here, and that was enough. I had at last lost all notion or grasp of time. Night or day, the whiteness was there, white shapes moving around me. It was much later that I heard what had happened to me during that time, how I had spent my time and how much time had been spent there.

Before I record this, or summarise my record, I want to ask something. . . . It may not be very clear.

If you have an animal (say a dog) which continually runs into the fire, leaps in front of cars or trucks, cannot balance on walls, incurs again and again the whip or boot; if this animal (or dog) is so accident-prone or stupid that it simply cannot learn to lead a contented and well-ordered life, what do you do with it? Do you diagnose it as—being deficient in feeling pain? And train it, accordingly, to keep out of danger? Perhaps. But if this dog patently does feel pain, if its whole life is one minor or major agony after another, if it yelps and howls with its broken bones, how do you train it then? I suppose you don't. You put it out of its agony and after a decent interval take on another, preferably of reasonable pedigree and straight from its mother's teat.

So begin again: for dog read human being. If you have a human being, innocent, surrounded by love and certain moderate privileges . . . but that doesn't lead anywhere either. Which human being is innocent, who analyses and pasteurises the love, what is privilege? What I am getting at is, how can a human being be taught happiness? Even that isn't accurate. How can a human being be taught to recognise the conditions for happiness, achieve those conditions and successfully live with them? I believe there are postal courses. There are gods promising eventual success; but where there are gods there are martyrs. There are philosophies and movements, sciences and superstitions all devoted to this end: but each of them creates heretics, victims, schisms, traitors, burnings, decapitations and an imposed sense of guilt. Amorality, then, anarchy, hedonism? Quite possibly but for these you need a rigid conscience to overcome, a repressive regime to overthrow and a warm climate. Imposed liberty is even worse than guilt. Guilt at least creates art. Dutiful liberation is a dead end, the barbiturates, the gas, the sword-sharp safety razor.

To go back to an old belief, drummed into me by people I can't remember: certain individuals are attracted to pain, have an ability actively to suffer and endure extraordinary agonies, most of them painstakingly created by themselves. It sounds very convincing and may, in certain extreme cases, be true. Pain certainly begets pain, and I suppose you can get a taste for it in the end. It's true that people are very adaptable and, once adapted, are hard to change, even for their own good.

From the moment I came to this place, I have encountered nothing but disaster (except for the period of my numbness, and then the interlude with the dog— even that makes me weep when I think of it). I have been spied on, betrayed, tormented by foolish entertainments, given insuperable tasks to perform; I have been abandoned, tortured with promises, and finally turned over, bound hand and foot, to the Director—by the very man in whose body I once swam, small as a pinhead, with a billion others. Did I bring all this on myself? For God's sake, or my own, am I to blame? A monotonous voice answers "Yes" to all these questions. I think it is misleading me.

What about the slings and arrows of outraged fortune? What about circumstance, cause and effect, chance, means without end and lack of meaning? What about fluke, luck, accident, acts of god? What about destiny? I remember (though it may be a dream) tidying a shoe cupboard while asking myself questions of this sort. I remember dreaming that the idea of personal responsibility belittles life, reduces its dignity. I don't, however, remember dreaming of any alternative.

The question is asked, though of whom, I don't know. In the white West Wing the white shapes had no doubts whatever. They looked me over after Gondzik took me there, listened to various reports and made their diagnosis: I was obviously hell-bent on self-destruction and the time had come to put a stop to it, to wrench me round and set me in another direction.

In order to get me out of my bad habit of suffering, they repeatedly convulsed me with many electric volts. Although their firm belief was that the root of the trouble was in my unconscious, they paradoxically believed that if I wasn't conscious of the pain of these electric shocks, I wouldn't feel it. My body, I suppose, clenched its teeth and writhed in a momentary death throe; in fact every part of me except for my anaesthetised nerves must have suffered appallingly. It seems a little inconsistent, but was perhaps based on the well-known scientific theory of taking a hair of the dog that bites you. It obviously frightened me very much, for in a few moments I was conscious (before they put me under again) intense fear was my main symptom.

Together with this benevolent electricity, they gave me an incredible and constantly changing quantity of drugs.

Until I learned better, and became wily, I screamed quite openly at the pain these pain-killing drugs caused me. The white shapes hung over me, solicitous. They shook their white heads. It seems I puzzled them. More white shapes were called in. More drugs were prescribed. I stubbornly continued to suffer. If I slept too much, they woke me up. If I was too wakeful, they put me to sleep. If I was depressed (some sad memory, perhaps, such as the dog), they cheered me up. If I was too cheerful (it seems they thought that was possible), they depressed me again. If I remembered, they made me forget. If I forgot, they forced me to remember. All in all, I had never known such unhappiness or such exhaustion. I literally did not know if I was coming or going. My sense of survival made one last feeble attempt to save me, and succeeded. In the space of perhaps half a second, in less time than it took to swallow one of their equilibrium-restoring tablets, I learned how to act. My part, that of a grateful and reformed criminal, came to me as if by magic. I already knew it by heart. I had become an entertainer.

They were so grateful. It touched me. They switched off the electricity and reduced the drugs (most of those they still gave me I managed to secrete inside my cheek, or stuff into the pillow case, or on one occasion, drop into a nurse's tea). They did this with the relief of people whose necessary brutality had hurt them much more than it hurt me. They congratulated me for looking so much happier, being so much more tractable. They showed me off to each other, their prize exhibit. I am sure I was written down as an example of the efficacy of their treatment, and probably held up as a sign of hope to others whose vice was to be misfortunate. I basked in their self-approval. It was a non-stop performance, and there were moments when I felt very tired, but fear, thank God, kept me going.

I was allowed to sit up, and then to walk about a little. The nurses and doctors remained capped, gowned and masked, so I supposed I was still infectious. I didn't ask questions, in case they might think I was becoming too alert. One day they led me to the window and at last pulled up the white blind. I was looking down on a garden full of flowers, and the old woman was there, bending and straightening and snipping.

I knew they were watching me, so I pretended not to recognise her, though my heart had leapt, I'm sure, visibly. To disguise it, I yawned, and immediately they were at me: did I feel tired, sleepy, lethargic, bored, liverish? Although I laughed and said no, two virulent yellow tablets were brought and I was put straight back to bed. I had to hold them so long in my mouth that one of them disintegrated and my brain started chattering like an eldrich, but I kept my mouth shut until it had quieted down.

The sight of the old woman wasn't the only shock. The time of the year seemed to be exactly the same as on the day of my abortive escape. And yet I had been in the West Wing for what must surely be many months. Perhaps it was already next year. Perhaps they had allowed me to look out of the window as a kind of anniversary present. Perhaps I was a year older.

I asked for a mirror (that, surely, must be harmless) and looked at my unfamiliar face. It seemed, insofar as I could recognise it, a little younger, plumper than I remembered. Since learning to act, my health had obviously improved, I had begun sleeping soundly (with secret dreams) for the regulation eight hours, and eating my good, regular food with moderate appetite. I was also (so long as I continued to act) secure for once, so that there weren't the furrows of anxiety I had expected. I had put on weight, certainly. I asked meekly if I could be taught exercises, which I knew would be met by squeals of approbation from behind the gauze masks. You're even beginning to like yourself a little, they said. I believe that you could grow to put up with your dearest enemies if you had to live with them day in, and day out, for a lifetime.

Now I had to be very careful. They weren't altogether fools, these people. I knew that this was just the time, when I appeared to be almost cured, when they would pounce on any little backsliding, any faint tremor of what they called more (or less) than "normal" feeling. I wished they would do their final tests and get them over with. I didn't in the least want to leave the West Wing, now everything was so amiable, but on the other hand I couldn't keep up this charade forever. If the final tests were negative, they might leave me alone a little more often, I might be able to relax my face occasionally, even let my body slump into a rare, restful attitude of dejection.

So we watched each other like hawks, I behind my perpetual smile, they over their white yashmaks. I recognised the first test the moment it came.

"It's time you had some company, have a few friends in. Who would you like to see?"

Truth is always the best defence. I said, "I'd like to see the baby. You know. The young man." Did they imagine I'd be silly enough to say Gondzik or someone readily available, on the premises?

"Ah," they said, regarding me keenly. "That might be difficult."

I looked mildly inquiring.

"To begin with, we have no idea where he is. The last we heard, he was passing through Cochabamba. To go on with, it probably wouldn't be allowed."

I allowed my shoulders to shrug ever so slightly. I glanced round the room, smiling, as though something else had caught my attention. I was amazed to find in fact my sense of mourning was a little dulled; that I was genuinely curious as to the location of Cochabamba.

There was a pause that, in more social circumstances, would have been awkward. They murmured among themselves.

"Anyone else?"

The old woman, of course. But that was too dangerous. I pretended I was trying to think, reviewing the vast hoard of my acquaintances. I looked at them lovingly.

"I'm really very happy here—for the time being, of course.

Why don't you ask anyone you happen to see? Just tell them to drop in. Later on, I might have a small party."

I held my breath, while appearing to breathe calmly. They couldn't disguise their delight. Some of the nurses clapped their rubber-gloved hands and one doctor actually tore off his cap and threw it in the air, revealing a neat bald head. They crowded around me, a gaggle of albatross, flapping their shrouded arms, their eyes innocent and bright with pleasure. I thought for a moment they were going to carry me shoulder-high in a triumphal procession. One of the nurses actually kissed my cheek, as well as she was able. On my supper tray there was a glass of champagne and one young, deep red rose. The minute I was alone I examined its stalk. It had been cut carefully, diagonally, by an old woman.

* * *

Now they left me more often, trusting me. The sunlight filtered through the slats of the blinds, which I was allowed to pull up when I wished. They brought me an excellent cassette player. I lay in the white room, now mellowed with shadows, and listened to Mozart, Bach, Haydn, a little Schumann, Dave Brubeck, Mulligan, Monk, Vivaldi. I had no opera, no oratorios, no vocals of any sort. The gentle and ordered music, prescribed by myself, washed my mind. I lay with my eyes open, breathing softly, waiting for the next simple ordeal.

But it surprised me. There was a scratching on the door. I was immediately upright, trembling. The dog, they had rescued or revived the dog! Nobody ever knocked, they glided straight in, since I was their property. I waited, a turmoil of fear, hope, uncertainty. I knew I couldn't fool the dog, and that if I responded to her excitement I would be done for. If I hugged her, ran about the room, willingly sacrificed my slippers, they would be out with their drugs for sublimation and masochism in no time at all. The scratching was repeated, now not with nails but knuckles. My disappointment was overwhelming. I lay back on my pillows, staring hard in order to dry my eyes. My throat was so choked that I couldn't speak for a few moments. Then with some effort I called, "Come in."

At first I didn't recognise him, the slight, diffident person who slipped through a very small opening in the doorway. He stood there, head bent, hair hanging, hands in pockets. I wondered anxiously whether the young man, who had been dark and tall and resilient, had in some way shrunk on his travels, become fair, hollow-cheeked and riddled with thought. I said, "Hullo."

"I'm Simon. You probably don't remember."

"Of course." I spoke very gently. "Did they ask you to come?"

"Well. They put up a notice."

"But you were the only one who wanted to come."

"I don't know. I came, anyway."

"I'm glad."

He came across the room and stood by my bed, looked at me very gravely.

"Are you all right?" he asked.

"Yes, thank you."

"Good."

He looked round the room. Any clothes, I thought, would be too big for him. He decided on an upright chair, fetched it and carried it to my bedside. He mounted it and sat cross-legged, observing me with a slight frown as though he were about to begin some lecture or discourse. He was, however, silent. I felt extraordinarily pleased.

"I thought you were the dog."

"Really?"

"They took her away and put her down. Humanely, of course."

"I'm sorry." There was a long silence. He seemed to be puzzling. After a while he smiled for the first time, an amazing transformation. "Then why did you think I was the dog?"

"I don't know."

He nodded. The quality of silence in the room had changed. It was like the silence that comes when an irritating noise is over.

"They said I wasn't to stay too long," he said.

"What's happening over there?"

"Do you really want to know?"

"Not really."

"So will you tell me when you are tired?"

"All right."

"Perhaps you should shut your eyes."

I shut my eyes. He perched on the chair. At first, to make sure, I opened my eyes very slightly, saw him blurred through my lashes and motionless. After a while I turned my head to one side (towards him) and lay blind. He stayed. He must surely have been uncomfortable. That was his business. I wanted to put out my hand without looking, but didn't dare to move. The hour, or the morning, or the afternoon or evening, flowed away. At last he said, "I should go now."

"Very well."

"I'll come again tomorrow."

"Thank you."

He unfolded himself, replaced the chair neatly.

"I'm glad you're all right."

I watched him go to the door.

"Do you know where Cochabamba is?" I asked.

"Of course," he said.

When he had gone I lay alone, with no audience, smiling.

14

He came the next day. Folded up on the fifteen by eighteen inches of the chair seat, he stayed longer (or did it seem not so long?). They were quite content to leave him alone with me. He was, after all, old enough to be the father of my grandchild. On this occasion (I think) he told me that he had come to this place on the recommendation of some distinguished person. This person had come into his kitchen one day and taken him away. I had a very clear picture of Simon's kitchen, which I never verified: it was long and narrow, with dirty coffee cups in the sink and many packets of wheat germ, wild rice, organic cereal and the like. Also organic spaghetti, if there can be such a thing. I noticed later, when he started eating with me, that he left most of his food untouched on the plate. I was appallingly tempted to tell him to finish it up. The waste distressed me, and of course he needed the good nourishment. In ways like this, insignificant and vitally important, Simon set me to learn some of the most difficult and valuable lessons of my life (or so it seemed at the time). Going against all my training (at the house, I suppose) I realised that I must never for an instant look after him, only towards him. I was to learn a new language: humility without resentment, pride without cruelty, strength without tyranny. It seemed at first as though it would be as easy as walking through a shadow and emerging, transformed, on the other side. But there were well-disguised periods of hopelessness, when I thought I could never learn even from Simon, even with all my heart and by heart. It was a question of beginning again from a long distance. In the times of despair, when I lay with a happy smile on my face, I told myself too late, too late.

But at first it was so simple. I lay in or on the bed. He sat on the chair. We talked (or I talked?) in a hushed torrent, often stopping abruptly, one stream blocked only to find a way round, rush on in a different direction knowing that eventually there would be a way, that if you were saying "go" you probably intended to say "come," that the truth would be reached somehow, that direction was only approximate. While the words poured, hesitated, stopped, veered, he put his hand on my bare foot, his hand smaller than my foot. Foot and hand prayed, sole to palm, fingers and toes mingling, exploratory. My foot became a separate person, as it was when I was a child and my feet crept cautiously through the tucked-in bedclothes, looked about for danger, crept farther, saw enemies and rushed back under the secure covers. The torrent became calmer, attention now moving to hand and foot. The torrent slowly, very slowly, diminished, flowed sluggishly between long banks of silence. My foot, his hand, spoke. Our eyes grew heavy. I reached out, almost languid, reaching down into still water. He came to me in one easy movement, as though we had overcome all obstacles of physical impossibility; it was no longer necessary to get up or walk, sit or lie down. His mouth was wide, composed, and soft as pressing one's lips gently against the soft flesh of one's inner arm (as I have seen children do, for comfort). I held his hair away from his face. The face, in trance, was beautiful, hair held back by the heavy water, eyes closed against the gentle push of the water, body moving fathoms deep, in its element. I joined him (I was afraid) clumsily. But in my heart, at least, I remembered.

Afterwards, as they say: it seems to be cheating, but what else is there to say? There is a time of silence to me more valuable than any words in any language in any world. Yes, we fucked. You want to know how? It goes like this . . . But that's so ridiculous, so pathetic. Everyone knows how it goes (even you, who fuck only in dreams, know the basic mechanics of the thing). Why strain with tormented words, with a mounting hysteria of frustrated words, where in fact there is silence? I admit it's by no means dead silence, because silence is recognisable only by the sounds that break it: the movement of submarine grasses; one bird; the thunder of a twig moved by an ant, the deafening flight of two butterflies in the sunlight. Even those words are too many and too inaccurate. Accuse me of sentimentalising. I hear no evil, see no evil, speak no evil. I am drowned on the bed of the ocean, I can't hear you.

* * *

He came every day, still slipping in through the door as though he had no right there, yet supremely confident that he had every right. I was examined, and did my exercises, and correctly answered all questions, before he came; from then on they left us alone. One evening they laid two places on my supper table and—the nurse's eyes merry, I thought, over the mask—brought us a bottle of wine. From then on he stayed until it was time for sleep, the time for sleep growing later and later so that often when he walked away (not lingering, or even looking back), I would be sprawled half-conscious, conscious only of the swift, no-nonsense departure out of me, and out of the room.

I have seen, to my amazement, a premature infant that I could hold on the palm of my hand, its skeleton hardly larger and no coarser than the skeltons of thrushes I would bury as a child. I adored, with a kind of adoration,

Simon's bones, the hip and spine and collar, the wrist (between my third finger and thumb), the separate ribs. I explored them with astonishment, my own bones feeling like cudgels in comparison. And yet, because this apparent fragility was powered by such a commanding, demanding, authoritative and sensitive instrument, it was tough and resilient as steel. There was no snapping him, no crushing him in the vice of my legs and arms. The vice, trembling, loosened. He was whole. It was he who encircled, encompassed and embraced me. It was he who orchestrated the laughter, the silences, the smiles, the sighs, moans, whimpers, the ultimate crescendo; he who made it all lucid. When I thought of suitable men, with their great thighs and chests labouring and vastly overlading their pitiful equipment, I grinned against his white neck, kissing it without moving my lips, all down the length and up to the bone behind the ear and across the hard apple that no man has been able to swallow. He delighted me. Therefore I was delighted.

But as a preliminary, and because we needed it, we talked. As though we had all the time in the world. It was very hard to imagine him as a little boy, since it was hard to imagine him surviving at that size; but I began to see a shadowy picture of someone who read about heroes (any hero, though he detested the dogged patience of Robert Bruce) and was supported and encouraged by wealth, shrewdness and ambition. Not surprisingly, he had a passionate desire to change the world. The world needs changing. He had, this eccentric exquisite, been beaten up and jailed by thugs of all persuasions: emerging jaunty, I imagined, a cigar clenched between his teeth, hands plunged into ample pockets which could contain a catapult or a gun. He had prayed with (heroic) gurus and found their feet muddy; submitted his clear wits to acid and other dangers (my heart contracting with concern) and collected them up again much enriched, or so he said. He had loved frequently, once deeply, though I didn't question him about this since it was his private concern. He imagined that he, too, was here in order to experience, in timelessness, the things he couldn't remember. I knew I was one of them, and this gave me great freedom and pleasure.

As for me, I told him about myself up to the time when I started running away from you. After that, I said (leaping centuries) I came to this place. I told him about Strewelpeter, the little boys dipped in the ink pot, the great big scissors man, the child who withered away and became a mere thread in the ground marked with a cross. I told him about the schools, in and out of which I had moved with such bewildering regularity, never getting further than fractions. I presented myself to him as a child he could never know, a child I had forgotten. And it was true. I was a child. I became childish. We played together, I and my father and son, he and his mother and daughter, the whole lot of us silly with enjoyment.

We began to play games about the future. Incarcerated in my room, it was good to escape.

"Tonight," he said masterfully, "I'm taking you to the fair."

"The fair?"

"You will see, as we approach in my powerful Rolls, the ferris wheel, the ups-and-at-'ems, the dodgems and doo-dahs glittering all green in the summer night. You will be very excited—"

"I will."

"But rather tired. Having parked the Rolls without effort—"

"And locked it."

"We amble slowly, probably arm in arm, towards the gay scene, I mean of course the scene of gaiety."

"The fair."

"Precisely. What do you say?"

"I say how remarkably quiet it is. No music. Just the wheel going round and the carrousels. All without music."

"Isn't that rather a pity?"

"No. The music of fairs is a din. We can do without din."

"All right," he said, gnawing judicially at a match end. "Our first stop is the agricultural implements, which include washing machines—"

"Why?"

"So that the farmers' wives can do their washing conveniently, without having to beat it against the stones. At this point I wonder whether you're going to be disappointed—"

"No, you don't. I do."

"We both do. But pass carelessly on to the cow shed—"

"Where great mink cows with huge haunches and eyes so soft and faun-like . . ."

"Shift in the straw, breathing heavily, shitting without discretion."

"And the calves are alone, lying down in their stalls or tottering about, except for one, which sucks from its mother great gulps of sweet hot milk."

"Enough of the cows."

"No, let's stay."

"Enough. Fantastic delights are in store for us. We idly inspect the jewellery made by gypsies in a lay-by off the motorway. You, being generous and rich, decide to buy me some trifle. A ring, I think."

"I want to buy you a chain to go round your neck."

"Of course you do, but save that as a more suitable encumbrance for your son. A ring would be better."

"All right. A ring. But they'll all fall off you."

"They're embossed with the heads of superannuated astronauts, so I decline the offer. We hurry now—"

"Wander."

"Hurry to the balloons. You make a great fuss, of course, about the exact balloon, which has to be extracted from an enormous bunch and is naturally in the middle. At long last—"

"You have waited with infinite patience."

"The green balloon is attached to yards and yards of

string and bobs about miles over your head while you clutch the end of the string greedily."

"Greedily?"

"In case the balloon should escape. You then have an insane desire, balloon and all, to visit the Witches' Castle—"

"I don't! I don't! I'm terrified of the Witches' Castle!"

"Exactly, that's why you want to see it. You're obsessed, passionately, by the idea of having slimy rags slapped in your face while travelling at one mile an hour in the pitch dark." He sighed deeply, throwing the match end in the direction of the ashtray. "Naturally, I humour you."

"You're telling too much of the story. And you're wrong. We watch the children falling about on the huge trampoline—"

"Water bed."

"Nonsense, they'd puncture a water bed. They jump and fly and swim in the waves—"

"You can't have waves on a trampoline."

"And leap on the trampoline. They look so pretty with their hair flying and knickers flashing, I don't want to leave them. But you have other plans. You want to visit the Witches' Castle!"

He took a breath, held up his hand to demand silence, but I went on pell-mell. "It's such a performance, I have to haul down the balloon and anchor it to your shoe with absolutely no faith that you've got the weight to keep it there. And the trucks clatter away into the tunnel with banshees wailing in dreadful ruins and flashing lights on mountain tops and the graves delivering up their dead and Götterdämmerung—"

"And the slimy rag slaps you in the face and you scream—"

"Don't." I could hardly speak for laughter and terror. "They'll think there's something wrong."

"And cower in my shoulder and scream and clutch me. That part of it is very pleasant."

There was a silence, but I wanted to get on with it, to know what happened next. "Go on," I urged gently.

"Well." He frowned down his nose, steepling the white pointed fingers. "What do we do next? Shoot the Chinese? Hoopla?"

"You shoot."

"But I want to win."

"I want you to win because you so much want to win."

"However. I don't."

"Then I kiss you in front of everybody in order to say it doesn't matter. And we pass by the weight-guesser."

"Who can't possibly guess your weight so you get landed with a revolting creature made of electric blue nylon. You win a prize."

He shook his head, considering. "No. The weight-guesser picks on you. "'You—the young lady with the balloon!'"

"But I don't go, of course."

"You don't. So he says. 'What about your father, then?' I shake my head—"

"And he says, 'Who shakes his head like a little girl.'"

We sat, smiling with pleasure. I moved over quietly, and sat at his knee. I rested my head on his knee.

"Go on. Go on."

"We inspect the awful contrivances for being whirled through space. But you say you don't like being turned upside down, not by a machine. This finally makes me laugh, so I hold the back of your neck, like this . . ."

"No, no. The story."

"All right. We mount the ferris wheel. With some trepidation on my part."

"But you don't show it. They bolt us in, and soon we're high . . . high among the stars . . ."

"There are no stars. It's starless."

"Then the night is plush, indigo plush. And as we go round and round and round and round—"

"The balloon accompanies us gallantly."

"I lean back, very far back, and watch the wheel going round backwards overhead."

"But—"

"Quiet." I was caught up in a vision. "The green cars come up and sail over my head, feet sticking over the edge of some of them, sometimes an arm flung out. The struts of the wheel and the elaborate engineering, sometimes they all disappear and there's just the sky, then into the sky comes a green car and another green car and another green car, and they plunge away down and there's nothing but sky. I wish I could show this backwards revolving, orderly revolving, everything upside down, all green and brilliant, I even forget you."

"I'm sad, I'm happy."

"My neck aches."

"And then suddenly you decide you've had enough. 'Stop! Stop!' you cry. 'Stop the wheel!' But it won't stop."

"It goes on forever. We're trapped. We'll go mad."

"Naturally, if you order the wheel to stop, it should stop. But oh no, round and round it goes, you growing frantic and forgetting me—"

"Stop the wheel!"

There were footsteps outside the door, a brief knock, a shrouded face with anxious eyes. Automatically I had leapt up, ran a few steps from Simon.

"Are you all right?"

"Yes. Yes." My laugh was too nervous, I had forgotten everything. "Of course. We were just playing . . . a game. . . ."

The eyes hardened. "I think you should go to sleep. Would you like a tablet?"

"No, thank you. Thank you."

The eyes moved to Simon, who said, "I'll go."

I implored him: not for a minute. The door shut disapprovingly, almost a slam.

I collapsed at his knee, horrified to find I was crying.

"Damn them, oh damn them, I was so happy."

He leant forward, stroking my hair, trying to turn my

face, troubled. "She's right, you should go to bed, I'll leave now."

"No, don't, please don't." Don't desert me, I'm frightened, I stopped acting, they've found me out. But I didn't say this, still clinging to my new language, which had no word for "demand."

"In a minute, then."

"All right." A long silence. He stroked my hair, kissed it, stroked it with his cheek. "Could you just finish the story . . ."

"Well . . ." His voice was quiet. "The wheel stops of course. It was always going to. We're rather tired now. Also I think we want to go to bed." He took me across the room and undressed me while he talked, folded back the bedcovers, guided me in, covered me. "We walk back through the fairground. I have a picture of you pinned to my heart."

"To where?"

"My heart." He slid his hand inside his jacket, showing the location of his heart. "We walk through the parking lot calling 'Car? Car?' but very softly. The Rolls clears its throat in a diffident sort of way, indicating that it's ready and waiting. I unlock your door and put you inside."

"I unlock yours," I mumble, "from the inside."

"We glide off into the night. I say that if you're not going to wear your seat belt—"

"Never."

"You might as well sit closer to me. You sit closer to me. And soon you sleep, soon you sleep."

I slept. When he left, after this fantastic excursion, I whimpered a little. For the first time for days or months, they came to look at me in the night.

15

I knew that there would be difficulties. And I suppose if the difficulties were traced right back to their antecedents, I could have been to blame. I lost my head with Simon, forgot my self-imposed training. And the reason I lost my head was . . . an unconscious longing for decapitation? It's an absurd and (even if true) insignificant explanation.

The next morning, after breakfast and before the exercises, they came to examine me intimately. A stretcher was wheeled in, to which were attached chromium stirrups. Then the doctor, whom I remember in his moment of exuberance as bald, was given a plastic glove out of a sterilised envelope. He inserted his gloved hand into me and investigated, while staring expressionless out of the window, my inner sex, sensitively probing and testing the route that Simon and his seed had so often taken. Presumably he mentally noted clues, fingerprints, any litter or small treasure that Simon had left on the way. Finally he withdrew his hand and peeled off the glove, which was received by a nurse with a look of devotion. They weren't talking very much that morning and their eyes were sombre.

The woman who taught me the exercises and supervised my performance had dead black hair (for some reason she didn't have to be covered), the body of a dancer and a face of dark granite. She had told me early on that she was nearing seventy, and I had been properly impressed. That day she came later than usual and I was impatient, thinking that Simon would be kept waiting. She was wearing a scarlet leotard and black net tights. Of all the people in the West Wing, she was the least friendly. That morning I thought there was something new about her, a kind of weariness and scorn.

We began as usual, breathing and praying. During the praying period I thought of Simon and the ferris wheel and smiled, mysteriously contemplating. Then we plodded along with the stretch and bend. In the periods of relaxation I squinted down my arm at the marbled vinyl of the floor, which seemed to stretch endless and glassy, as though I were an ant.

She came and stood over me, legs apart, hands on her scarlet hips.

"Now," she said, "we're going to have a little test."

"Test?"

"Of endurance."

Now that was one thing I was good at. I could endure anything, so long as it was physical. Little did she know how I had subjugated (in my own fashion) that house.

"Fine," I said. "What do I do?"

"Lie flat. Legs straight. Feet together. Hands at your sides."

I did so.

"Now slowly raise both feet eight inches off the floor. Are you ready?"

This was child's play. Staring solemnly at the ceiling (in case she didn't think I was taking her seriously), I raised my straight legs, toes pointed towards the future. She glanced at her gold watch, no larger than a penny, on a thin gold band round her wrist.

"All right?"

"Of course."

She sat down, cross-legged, in one movement. She rested

the backs of her hands on her knees, first finger and thumb together. She stared over me at nothing.

I lay with my feet eight inches off the floor. She appeared, straight-backed, her face unflinching, to be surrounded by coma. After what may have been three or four minutes her eye flicked towards me like an adder's tongue. I remained serene. The muscles of my vagina and other inner passages clenched like biceps. My legs started trembling.

Still she sat, a corrupt squaw who had been given, through some nefarious trading with evil spirits, the body of a young woman. My knees were bending and I straightened them savagely. Small fires broke out, smouldering at the base of my spine. My most treasured possessions were congested with pain. But I knew that the moment I cried out, allowed my legs to fall to the ground, they would be in with their syringes and trays of blue and turquoise and black licorice allsorts. They would forbid me to see Simon. They would have proved that I could still suffer. I tried to force myself into a state of mind in which suffering was of no consequence. I wandered with Simon through the woods, taking him to tea with the old woman, who wouldn't understand. I watched the dog tussling a stick, the baby tottering unsteadily across a room, bumping into the furniture. My eyes, I felt, were bulging with these efforts. Sweat ran down my face and I couldn't brush it away. I wanted to explain "It's rather hot in here," but for once (unlike other times when I had been in extremis) I couldn't manage the trite phrase, the feeble joke. The woman, I saw (out of the misted corner of my eye), was staring at me now. She seemed to be at a loss.

"Had enough?"

I managed a very slight movement of my shoulders, a faint parody of indifference.

She walked across the room, silently, out of my vision. She walked back again. She was defeated.

"All right. Relax now."

I wasn't going to let my legs tumble. I lowered them slowly, I hoped elegantly, until the heels brushed the floor, then rested. Everything inside me had collapsed, walls broken, paths destroyed, pain flaring steadily. I looked up at her with contempt, finding contempt from somewhere.

"You're an extraordinary woman," she said.

"Yes," I said. "I know."

When she had gone, presumably to make her report, I crawled to the bed, climbed onto it with my last strength, lay on my stomach with arms hanging on either side of the bed (which was narrow and hard and which Simon, by some crafty display of body and limbs, could totally monopolise). When the door inched open and he came in (I had passed the test, I had passed) I could do no more than look up with my eyes from the Procrustean bed.

"Are you all right? What's the matter? What's wrong?"

"Nothing."

"You're crying."

"I'm not crying."

The lie, like all the (few) lies I told him, didn't even attempt to be the truth. My face was covered in tears. But I told him I was not crying out of necessity: for if I were crying, he would be troubled, need to know why, we would have to stay with the pain instead of setting out on more interesting and important enterprises. And for the first time, with my back torn open and my organs a mess of offal I resented his coming and going, his lack of responsibility, his detachment and youth. Why did they have to inflict this on me? Why not, at least a little of it, on him? He regarded me with severe worry, his brows drawn together, some words (but what words?) struggling to be spoken.

"I'd like you to go on with the story," I said.

After a moment's hesitation, he gave in, moved the chair to my bedside, began to think of the story. Now I wanted him to ask me why I had been crying, I wanted him to take charge of the pain. But, believing a story was what I wanted, he began with his once upon a time.

It wasn't a success. Neither of us had our hearts in it. The fact was that this woman in grave discomfort and this helpless boy were alone in a room, and nothing to be done about it. The story trailed away, and after a while he went to find a chess set. We played chess in silence, a stalemate. I felt he was restless in the room, wanting to pace about or go and play with his friends. I couldn't touch him, but wanted to be gently stroked and kissed. I did not say to him "I want to be gently stroked and kissed," and he, feeling in awe of me, stayed far away on his chair. In the evening he read aloud to me some myth about the beginning of the world. It was beautiful, he read well (something of an actor on the side). But the physical distance between us was a breeding ground for weeds, they grew higher even though I could have stopped them, but I was too tired for gardening. He left early.

The next morning (I dreamed, but certainly not of you) I woke early and felt better. The relief of feeling better was enormous. I swung out of bed and pulled up the blinds with a clatter. The colours of the flowers were hazy with dew and mist. I opened the screens and leaned far out, testing my stomach and pelvis on the sill, lifting myself on taut and healthy arms. I saw a grass path I had never seen before, a straight path continuing as far as I could see, flanked with pergolas and small box hedges. I wondered when they would let me go outside. I wanted to walk with Simon along the grass path, which must surely end in a stone seat covered in bird lime, a shady isolated place where we could kiss and touch each other and softly sigh with anticipation, playing at lovers. I felt suddenly resentful that we were kept here, away from the eyes of other people, with no plans for the future. I felt (guiltily) resentful at Simon's placid acceptance of the situation. Why didn't he tell them I must go out? Why did he so obediently agree to stay indoors all day, to visit me like a health visitor instead of staying with me in my bed? Why, a more rational voice enquired, didn't I demand a larger bed? At the sight of the grass path, I had remembered the future and forgotten the past.

Though I did not altogether forget the lessons I had been learning. When he arrived, therefore, I didn't welcome him with an army of words and questions. We didn't even wait for the usual conversation: for the time being we knew enough about each other. He came straight to me, a speechless and for the first time violent meeting. It seemed as though we had been apart for too long. He held me down. For the first time, I damaged his pale skin. For the first time, I didn't lovingly and lingeringly unlatch the leather belt, I ripped it open. His pride, my joy, reared up out of all proportion to the slender body. He plunged straight and deep, holding me closely. The pain was the most sharp, the most desolating I had ever experienced. I was impaled on driving steel. "Sinner!" it screamed. "Sinner!" The pain yelled with laughter at its trickery and awful punishment. "Sinner! Sinner!"

I was too stubborn to cry out. I stuffed my arm between my teeth, praying that he thought the stifled whimpering came from pleasure. They had succeeded well. Pleasure was done for. When he leapt in me, I didn't feel it, the pain numbed all other feeling. When he left the bed there was no swamp of warm, lubricating blood, but evil, brilliant spots, as though my cunt had tried to stop itself crying.

I didn't tell him at first, afraid of introducing such crude and unmanageable reality, afraid of frightening him, of losing him. Unable to see into his skull, I was under-estimating him perhaps. Of course I wasn't going to tell the doctors or nurses (who of course already knew), I wasn't going to give them the satisfaction. For some days we went on as before, playing, talking, laughing a great deal, loving. But there was a hectic edge to my tenderness for him. I soared dangerously, with those scarlet spots, like a tubercular romantic. I was too happy, too greedy: and, when he left, too cast down. I dreaded his coming into me, felt bitterly cheated, trying to give all my pleasure as well as his own.

Finally, exacerbated with every renewed attack of love, I told him about the examination, the test of endurance and the pain.

He said, "I wish you'd told me before."

"I didn't want to frighten you."

"I'm worried. Not frightened."

I reached for his bones, swept him with my hair, the frown smoothed away, he stopped being worried. I took him into my mouth, he spilled in my mouth, over my face, I annointed him with himself. We smiled and whispered, planning to market this rare substance in delicate face-masks and shampoos for beauty parlours. My body, in spite of its prohibited area, served us well. He took me far back to childhood, before procreative sex was born. He pored over me as delicately, with as intense a concentration as someone turning over the pages of a rare book, lifting the tissue covering the plates, tracing the outlines with gentle fingers. His tongue traced me as though I were an oyster shell: as though I were his own mouth, in which he was exploring inner cheeks and small, intricate cavities. When we kissed we brought home new flavours imported from abroad, tart liqueurs and spices, civet and musk, the taste of rare and exotic secretions. The nurses' eyes were puzzled, even dismayed. We seemed happy.

We were not children, but we were forced to be. I thought that in time the damage would repair itself and we would be able to grow up again. In time. But how much time? They told me Mrs. April would be coming to see me in a few days, and I was terrified. That meant that having apparently survived this last endurance I was to be pronounced cured and taken away. I had no doubt of this. But the terror of the electricity and the drugs was greater. I daren't pretend I wasn't well enough.

"When we get back there—what shall we do?"

He considered a moment. "I don't know."

I felt a dull, unconcentrated fear. "Well. What do you think?"

He considered again. "I suppose . . . we shall go on as we did before."

"How can we do that? There was no before."

He grinned, with faint irony. "Then we shall have to make one."

But I knew the truth so well that I could try, much as

134

dying people are said to repeat the Ave or whatever prayer they know, one last question: "Why don't we leave? Both of us."

"With you? I couldn't do that."

I paused carefully. "Why not?"

"Because . . ." He thought for a while, then looked at me honestly. "You know why."

The rejection was so clear, so clear, so simple, that it was almost painless. I sat quiet, trying to see my fate down the long grass path. He sat quiet, I didn't know what he was trying to do. Then he smiled.

"What are you smiling at?"

"I don't know." He turned his smile towards me, it seemed full of trust. "I guess I'm happy."

He was happy. Because I had asked him to leave with me, even though it was impossible. What a remarkable happiness, achieved as easily as tossing a coin and buying a newspaper, as easily as picking a pleasant flower. I didn't say anything else, and even my fear was nursed in a desultory fashion, sleeping most of the time.

We made love in the afternoon, and in the evening he sat on his chair. It was colder, and he wrapped himself in one of my blankets, completely shrouded except for the melancholy face. As though this would make it easier (though what, neither of us really knew) he became a little petulant for the first time, babyish, even going so far as to irritate me. I felt a thousand years old, tired and unapproachable. I didn't bother to charm him. In the days when the baby, whoever he was, came back or home, I would welcome him with lank hair, a face destroyed with exhaustion, aching all over. So, that night, I lay passive, being who I was. And for the first time I sent him away, and for the first time he looked back when he reached the door. I could have opened my arms, but what was the point? He left. I lay for a time, then switched out the light and slept.

In the morning Mrs. April, as I knew she would, arrived.

"Well, dear, how nice to see you. Ready to go?"

"Mrs. April. I want to ask you something."

"Of course." She was all attention.

"What shall I do about Simon?"

There was a long silence. I think she had been prepared for this question, but now didn't know how to answer. She pressed her hands together, looking down at the floor, looking up to me. "Simon has gone."

"Yes."

"It is very important . . . I think . . . that you now forget."

"But if I forget. Won't it happen all over again? The love. The separation."

"Not necessarily." Here she was on firmer ground. "I think the experience itself is . . . indelible." She seemed to apologise for using such a formal word. "You just have to forget, in order to go on."

"You mean pretend to forget?"

She smiled naughtily. "If you put it like that. I think you can choose, now, what is . . . best . . . for you to remember."

"Yes. I understand."

"You have done very well so far."

I was pleased. "Thank you. I tried very hard."

"I know you did."

"Is Simon happy?"

"He will be. In a day or two. He's gone to stay with his peers."

I got up and went with her through long, white corridors, thinking that Simon had walked this way twice a day, and must know it by heart. A car waiting for us, but it wasn't a very long journey. By the time we had reached the mansion I had already forgotten most of the things I have recounted here.

*   *   *

This is the past, there's no point in pretending that it isn't. I hope, however, (though I am not yet sure) that I can think of it without regret, guilt or remorse. I had been very happy, within my allowance. I hope that Simon, whom I loved, is living firmly, with certainty, unwounded and unafraid. My father, the end of my heredity, sang a song: in the fair vale of Clwyd in the days of my joy, e're the primrose was over I loved my slender boy. He was graceful as the willow, he was steadfast as the oak. Bitter tears wet my pillow for the plighted vows I broke. But I didn't make any vows. A vow annihilates itself. Once broken, it magically ceases to exist.

Fortissimo: brave Sir David came hunting, with houses and land. Though I cared not, I wed him—he was mine to command. I was queen of his treasure, I had homage everywhere. But my heart found no pleasure, and his love no dwelling there. This, even now, vaguely reminds me of a dream in which I plighted myself to you for thirty acres, thirty measures of land, and only the daffodils monotonously grew and died and disappeared and grew again.

This type of nostalgia is not, in fact, fitted to Simon. I know perfectly well that it wasn't all a bed of roses. There were times when our games palled, when one of us would refuse to play. At these times it was always the children who took over, leaving the archetypal parents with nothing to do but yawn and fidget and drink. There were sulks, stamps of the foot. Then I would leave them, these liberated generations in their fantasy playground, and go as far as I could into the frozen, desolate places of my own mind. It was cold and bleak there, not a soul in sight: arctic conditions would prevail until death. But after some calling and halloing, to-ing and fro-ing, touch and go, we would come back together, I would gently reprimand or be reprimanded (which I took badly, of course, since it came from my own mouth) and we would start again, rather self-consciously at first, bruised and confused by the trial separation.

This occasional failure of the idyll wasn't—I know this too—the only hazard. The parental Simon (didn't I pay enough attention?) was a formidable man. He could see, all at once, vast stretches of life, great land masses, huge horizons; these he would people (intently, frowning, tongue exploring upper lip) with a kind of compassion that was beyond my grasp. I was left behind on these expeditions of his, I felt myself to be a sailor's wife, simple, patient, knowing my place, which was a wharf on which I sat with hands clasped, gazing out to sea, a pretty picture of puzzled acceptance.

I know there were bitter disappointments in myself: when I couldn't learn (even though the learning was surely for my benefit, not his) to let go, say a casual good-bye. There were times when the knowledge that he didn't belong to me, that he would fly away on a crane and never come back, enraged me, baffled me, drove me momentarily mad.

I know all this, but forget it. He has been gone so long (and so properly, of course) that facts are hard to remember, even if I recognised that I could remember. The melody of the song—like those settings of Longfellow and Tennyson that worried me so much at one time—re-creates a sensation: the sensation, if I concentrate sufficiently, creates a state of mind. Simon for me is a sensation (compounded of an immeasurable history of sensation), and a state of mind. I don't feel that anything more is necessary.

PART
FIVE

16

I had hardly thought about my return, imagining everything would be just as I had left it; though I knew there would be an absence. My room, indeed, is precisely the same, picture crooked, fruit in fair condition, dressing tables in front of the three doors. Inconsistently, this amazes me. The sun shines as though it is still high summer, the shadows don't appear to move; when I sit in the upholstered rocking chair, the lily pond is still exactly in the centre of my line of vision, the deck chairs are dry on the terrace and before supper Leonora's laugh hacks mercilessly, just as before.

But I am beginning (at first without knowing it) that imperceptible separation from myself which, when completed, will be permanent.

Gondzik is away on business of some sort. That (after the terrible mourning for the dog, which soon ceases to be terrible) is a shock. For a short while, the place without Gondzik seems as though it should be unbearable. They say his visit is only temporary, and that he will soon be back. Elizabeth has returned, less limp, more nervous than before. Paul and Revlon have both gone: until I forget what it was like when they were here, I miss them. Dominic has isolated himself, seldom appearing, even for meals. He is, it seems, involved in something. Rowena has grown even smaller: she is marmoset eyes on a stick insect, grotesque.

But there are new visitors: a great square hunk of gum-chewing peasant, who sits and and cries quietly on the landing; three lean, secretive men with little eyes who form, with the homosexuals, a battalion. Their names are undistinguished: Adam and Hugh and Bill. It is hard at first to see the exact formation of the battalion, its allegiance or purpose. I am a stranger to them, although they may have heard about me. For a time I automatically try to live as I did before, and steer clear of them. It is hard, without Gondzik, without the dog. Without.

A wisp, a mere vapour of me at first, drifts down to the terrace to join the women, Rowena, Elizabeth, sometimes Leonora, and the silly blonde (still working her fingers to the bone). I believe that I totally have joined them, and naturally don't look up at my windows to see myself looking down. Anonymous among the women, I feel that there may be a suitable, if temporary, future.

I have forgotten the din of ancient Mondays. It is as though for a very long time I have lived a prolonged, exquisite Sunday evening, the fever of my life over and my work done. I have forgotten the imperious sounds of the house, the foetid smells, the stained lavatories, the slimy face flannels. I have forgotten that all this (and so much, so much more of the same) is the domain of women—or should I say, to be fair, those women who have been carried pro-testing over doorsteps and allowed themselves to be locked in. It is not simply that they discuss over and over again their own menstrual irregularities, abortions, obstetrical repairs, gynecological damage, wickedness of doctors, im-morality of psychoanalysts, difficulty or ease of obtaining popsocks or crotch-fitting tights, heartaches, past betrayals, immediately imminent rescues, hopes for and suspicions about and inevitable treachery of men. No. Having dis-cussed all these formidable items in relation to themselves and each other, they embark on them with fresh enthusiasm in relation to their friends, their daughters, their aunts' cousins, the women who told them once and the women who told them about. I begin to understand why Leonora's chief comment is that cheerless laugh; why she continues to fling herself at a man, any man, and demand immediate conversation; why, when she gets it, she has nothing to say.

Nevertheless, I stubbornly try to convince myself that, being so vastly out-numbered by masculine and feminine men, they are simply putting up some sort of makeshift womanly front. I ask whether there is any new scandal from the office. They remember something about—what was it?—the Director's wife having a hysterectomy, or was it that the widower Hathaway is said to keep his secretary (secretary, indeed!) working until late at night, until very late at night. If any of them have secret lives, or meet people in the gardens, they keep quiet about it—afraid, I imagine, of frightening the men by appearing neurotic or unusual. In fact they also seem to succeed in frightening themselves. Their eyes are constantly alarmed, they shake easily, bite their nails, jump at loud noises.

It might be possible in other circumstances to blame all this on the arrogance of the men; but the men are so pitifully lacking in arrogance. I know that Gondzik—if his fantasies are in any way based on fact—must have made a formidable enemy, forever pushing himself into their mouths as though feeding them with candy, patting their heads and giving them little treats of himself. However, they didn't have to put up with it, they could have hit back; and Gondzik, from all I hear, has been away a long time, even though he will shortly return. The women really have nothing to fear. Nobody oppresses or persecutes them. That, of course, is what they fear: the emptiness of indifference, the responsibility of finding themselves responsible for themselves, the lack of anyone to blame. They don't want to be women, they want to be leaders of men; but the men, tepid and timid, don't wish to be led, they can't stand to attention on command.

Much of my education, it must be obvious by now, is gained through my father's songs. Pretty Polly Oliver, the pride of her sex, is rousing and merry. He really only sings it to amuse me, having no deep feelings about it himself. The love of a grenadier her poor heart did vex. He courted her so faithful in the good town of Bow, then marched off to foreign lands a-fighting the foe. Sometimes I sing the next verse, leaving him to turn the pages. I cannot, sings Polly, rest single, nor false I'll not prove, so I'll list as a drummer boy and follow my love—peaked cap, looped jacket, white gaiters and drum, and marching so manfully to my true love I'll come.

We do the next bit together, clowning grief. 'Twas in the battle of Blenheim in a fierce fusillade, a poor little drummer boy was prisoner made. . . . But a brave grenadier fought his way through the foe, and *fifteen fierce Frenchmen* together laid low! Now my father takes over, simulating first tenderness, then riotous joy: He bore the boy tenderly in his arms as he swooned. He opened his jacket to search for a wound. "Oh Pretty Polly Oliver, my bravest, my bride! Your true love shall never more be torn from your side!"

The moral of this tale, I suppose, is that if you are outwardly disguised as a boy—though bearing your secret wound with fortitude—you will be rewarded with eternal life. I certainly identify a good deal with Polly Oliver, strutting about with my toy drum, blackened with the grime of battle, but I don't much like the end, and would prefer her to die a hero's death. In principle, the story interests me and is a subject well suited to social psychiatry courses, but bears little relation to the men and women in this place, who are not engaged in battle or love.

Bored and disappointed, I drift away from the women and go back to the pool. The women don't go there much, it is always the wrong time of the month, or they are self-conscious about their figures. The hard-worked blonde swims only at night in what she calls the nude.

It is at the pool—a shred of me, a paring of my dividing self, lying with head in the shade—that I discover the

144

nature and purpose of the battalion. Adam, Hugh, Bill and their retainers have taken the place over. They bask in the sun with all the indolence of replete emperors. They are surrounded, at a discreet distance, by prostrate sycophants, by sun oil and other unguents, small mirrors, decorative (unlike mine) towels, titbits and carafes of wine (so that they, like Gondzik, received certain privileges). Rings glitter on their indolent fingers, they wear fine gold chains and swimming trunks like careless fig leaves. Compared with them, I feel bulky and dowdy, but it doesn't matter, they are nothing to do with me.

A tap on my shoulder: a summons. Opening my eyes, I see Adam squatting on his heels beside me, head a little on one side, boyish and appealing as only a middle-aged man who has studied the gestures for over forty years can be. He is offering me a section of peach, both the peach and the smile seductive. "You look such a lonely little girl," he says in gracious explanation.

In a short while this fragment of myself—which I now begin to observe from the outside—joins the battalion in the guise (what possible qualifications do I have?) of an international sophisticate. The title and rank are theirs but this part self seems to know exactly what is required of it. It leaps expertly on double meanings, serves up saucy scandal at a moment's notice, appears to have a knowledge of perversity which quite astounds me. I realise that the battalion has made some sort of coup and (for the time being, and until Gondzik's return) has imposed their own autocratic regime on the old timeless, liberal muddle. The office, being in such dire straits, needs all the support it can get and turns a blind eye while feeding them with dainties. Their purpose (commendable, I would think, in the West Wing) is to extract every possible pleasure from life. To achieve this end, their justified means are always devious, often cruel, sometimes brutal. They are pledged to destroy (tinkling and glittering with glee) any form of lugubriousness, ugliness or mediocrity. Seldom bothering to move from their appointed thrones by the pool, they tease and torment until their victims blubber for mercy, readily offering any part of their bodies that may, on a whim, be thought appetising. It is because of them that the simple hunk cries on the landing. A devastated puritan, he can't endure it, and yet he must endure, and yet he can't endure. One part of him longs to throw itself down and be assaulted, torn apart by their meddling fingers; the other part weeps and prays and clings to memories of wheat and children. He hasn't yet learned (as I am learning) that these two selves can separate and lead their contradictory lives in freedom.

Sitting in my rocking chair (holding my innocence like an old, battered treasure, a threadbare toy, a holy relic), I see myself doing the most extraordinary things. My voice has become deep and sharp with viciousness. I laugh most of the time, particularly at misfortune. I am party to their schemes and plot some of their most outrageous enterprises. I put my body at their disposal, for there are times when even they feel that three orifices are better than two. The penis, prick, cock, their mighty emblem, is borne by me in triumph into foreign territories. Buttocks, bottoms, bums, backsides, arses and arse holes, the anus and the rectum, are pronounced divine, seats of ambrosia full of succulence. From my rocking chair, I gape with disbelief. But it is so. There will be no more children. The boys will be bought as slaves, the girls thrown away. Only the mothers, mummified even in life, will be allowed to survive, and they will be put into charming temples situated at a safe but accessible distance. It is an old, old story; but I, participating in it for the first time, appear to find it enthralling.

Even from the rocking chair, looking down towards the lily pond, I find it more intriguing than the plaintive dreariness of the women. Nevertheless, I am a woman. I see myself in bed with the crying man, helping to break down his defenses. (If George were here now, he would not be allowed to remain average.) "Don't!" I call out to myself. "Don't do it!" But I laugh and laugh, telling him secrets that will make him weep all the harder.

I see myself everywhere, on beds, divans, sofas, floors, tables, on grass and the spongy ground of the pine forests (he was dressed in shirt of doeskin, white and soft and trimmed with ermine, all inwrought with beads of wampum. He was dressed in deerskin leggings, fringed with hedgehog quills and ermine, and in moccasins of buckskin, thick with quills and beads embroidered. On his head were plumes of swansdown, on his heels were tails of foxes, in one hand a fan of feathers, and a pipe was in the other. Barred with streaks of red and yellow, streaks of blue and bright vermilion, shone the face of Pau-puk-Keewis. From his forehead fell his tresses, smooth, and parted like a woman's shining bright with oil and plaited, hung with braids of scented grasses). I see myself, intent with the others on some treachery or lechery, dancing and whooping through the pinewoods, catching obscenity, juggling it and throwing it high, gaudy with coloured ribbons. We run, we play tag, we fall in heaps of two, three, four on the ground and in a moment are up again, singing, carrying weapons. The moon is full, the lawn, where we shall stage whatever game we are going to play, is grey as ash, the statue in the lily pond supplicates. We pour out of the woods on to the lawn, running for the statue as though it were a maypole.

Adam arrives at the pond first. He leans on the wall, leans over, jabs something with a stick. He begins a clear, exuberant laugh. Hugh and Bill are close behind, they peer, jab, fall helpless against the wall, their heads thrown back, teeth gleaming. The others run faster. The only woman, I show a moment's petulance. I cry "Let me see, let me see, pigs, bullies, bastards!" I push between them, looking down into the pool.

Caught in the placid, folded lilies is an infant's body, naked, a girl. It is so small it could be lifted on the palm of my hand. It is bloated and black with drowning. After an interminable moment I turn away and walk with dragging feet back to the mansion. I pull down the blinds, but from my rocking chair I can hear their laughter diminishing into the woods as they carry away their prize.

* * *

But the office finds out. They have gone too far. The battalion is disbanded, Adam and Hugh and Bill stripped of their decorations, their adornments, their privileges and their power. They appear at breakfast with the grave, proper faces of punished schoolboys. They have been issued with ordinary clothes and someone has neatly cut Hugh's hair, which yesterday hung to his waist. They don't speak much, and avoid each other's eyes. When they do speak, their voices have broken; they murmur short, moderate sentences about passing the pepper and hoping Rowena slept well.

As for me, it is most extraordinary. I receive, by hand, a letter from the Director himself. Thanking me. Telling me I have done well. Asking me if I will go (when summoned) to the office and speak with Mr. Hathaway. Since seeing the floating infant, I have been entirely myself. Now, reading this inexplicable letter, the other part goes and sits in the rocking chair, rocking, gazing. Remembering.

The mind of the first part thinks it may find out what happened to them after they were caught, what went on in the office, why they weren't taken to the West Wing to be cured. Possibly destroying pleasure takes less time and effort than destroying pain. Or perhaps (the mind of the first part thinks) there was nothing, really, to be cured; nothing that a stern talking-to couldn't take care of, or six meaningful strokes of the cane. They turned out in the end to be quite ordinary men. Men are little boys at heart, the mind of the first part tells me; and boys will be boys.

But the mind and heart of the second part knows something different now. Firstly, that it has been divided and may well have to live alone in the end. Secondly, that there was a boy like a man, a man like a woman, a woman like a boy, a mother like a child, a father like a mother; a father of a mother, who shook his head like a little girl. Thirdly, this part now knows, with confidence, that these facts are indelible.

PART
SIX

17

Curiously enough (it seems to me curious), I worry about not having proper clothes for my promised or threatened interview with Hathaway. I spend a day washing, mending and ironing my dresses: even then, they are too florid, revealing too much or too little. Jeans, I feel, would be improper. I think of asking Mavis to help out: surely she could buy me a skirt, sweater and leather shoes somewhere? But I have no money and don't know what they use here for money. I compromise by shortening one of the dresses to knee-level. My legs are so tanned that they are quite decent. I can scrub my linen shoes with soap and water, stuffing paper into the toes so that they dry in some kind of foot shape. My hair has grown long and shaggy, so I experiment by drawing it back sharply and tying it in a knot. I look quite different, rather formidable, and shake it loose again with relief.

There is a knock on my door, and who should be there but Gondzik, with a little more grey in his beard, smiling all over.

"Hi," he says.

"Hi."

"It's good to see you. How've you been?"

"Fine." Plumbing it, I find my heart has sunk a little.

I don't want to be taken over again. I don't want to be told how bad I am, how much better I could be. I don't want my days planned, or to be owned. "You're back?"

"Not exactly. I've come to take you to Hathaway."

"You? How nice. I thought it would be . . . someone else."

"Who?" He's smiling at my silly ideas.

"I don't know."

"Well, then, are you ready?"

"Of course."

I know the way. It was on my map, which I left in the gardener's hut. Gondzik puts his hand on my shoulder, affectionately, as though he's arrested me.

As we go down the stairs, beneath the stained-glass window, thread our way through the heavy furniture in the hall, I ask him, "Have you been there all the time? I mean, in the office."

"Off and on. How was your stay in the West Wing?"

"Oh, it was . . . very interesting."

"Good. Good. We don't have many connections with the West Wing. I was worried."

"You mean the West Wing is"—I puzzled for the words, they came obediently—"outside your jurisdiction?"

"More or less." He steers me across the terrace, down the steps. I look up at my open windows. No one's there. "Hathaway will tell you, of course. But I'd just like to say, for myself—you did a great job."

"Did I?"

"The baby in the lily pond. We knew, of course, no one else would have thought of it."

"Thought of it?" I enquired stupidly.

"Brilliant. The West Wing must have done you a whole lot of good."

It's too ridiculous. *I* drowned the baby? *I* left it there for the battalion to catch and carry? I'm bewildered, outraged. And yet I have learned so well to act, that the actor in me congratulates herself: that would have been a clever thing to do, it would have been a master stroke

—if I had thought of it. So I stay silent. His hand on my shoulder is hot and heavy, even though I know it is a delicate hand.

We are making polite conversation. "How are things . . . in the office?"

"Difficult. We'll survive, of course."

"You work there now?"

He looks at me shrewdly, little eyes flicking sideways behind gold-rimmed glasses. "I always did."

"So you were . . . ?"

"An agent. Yes, you could call it that. It's vital. For security."

"Of course. For security." Did I really say that? Well, security is something I understand by understanding so well the lack of it. We all need security, safeguards, guardians, safe lodging, a holy rest and peace at the last. Perhaps that's where Gondzik is taking me.

"I'm taking you the long way," Gondzik says. "There's a short cut I'll show you later. Right by the West Wing, as a matter of fact."

"You mean along the path by the flower garden?"

"That's it. Take a left at the stone seat, you're at the side door."

"That's convenient."

But this time we go under the No Entry sign, with nothing to park or unload, our shoes on. The memory of the dog stabs me, cuts me in half. Did Gondzik, then, participate in the dog's death? I'm going to be received by the enemy. I will fling myself on Hathaway, beating him with my fists. I will spit on him, I will break his furniture, I will expose his immorality with the secretary. As for Gondzik, I will kill him slowly, scalping his beard, submitting him to dreadful agony. But the woman in the knee-length dress and clean shoes is quite proud to be walking under the No Entry sign, being saluted by guards. By accompanying Gondzik, she is given priority and admiration. She smiles prettily, saying "Hullo" because she doesn't know whether it's good morning or good afternoon.

The office is busy. People hurry to and fro, carrying papers. The muted thunder of electric typewriters comes from cubicles. An elevator takes us smoothly upwards, stops with a sigh of regret, always prevented from soaring on. We step out onto a carpeted corridor. There are plants in ceramic tubs. Gondzik knocks softly on a mahogany door whose neat brass lettering simply says 31. "Come in," the secretary calls, low-voiced. She is, of course, glamorous, dressed in pink. She welcomes me, even shakes my hand. "Mr. Hathaway will be *so* pleased." I smile haughtily, as befits (I think) both sides of my character.

Gondzik goes into the inner office first, asking me to wait a moment.

"We were so impressed," the secretary says. "To tell you the truth"—another confidence—"we knew long ago. I mean even before the play. You remember?"

"You knew what?" I know I can afford to sound offended.

"Why, that with a little assistance . . ." She looks up, smiling, as Gondzik beckons me inside.

Hathaway (of course) sits at a larger desk, his back to the window. He gets up and advances on me, hand outstretched. Handsome, with an unnaturally even tan, grey curls just slightly dishevelled, a well-cut suit, collar and distinguished tie. "I'm so very pleased to meet you. Please sit down. Would you care for a drink? Gondzik, the drinks. Are you well? Are you happy? I must say you look quite . . . stunning. Gondzik, you never told me the lady was stunning. Gondzik likes to give me these pleasant surprises. Quite frankly, I was expecting . . . but never mind, all's well. You've been at the pool a great deal, of course. You must tell me all about it. We must have many long talks. Cigarette? Comfy?"

During all this, slightly dazed, I sit and regard the room. It is large and pleasant. Flowers (brought by the devoted secretary) everywhere. A large leather-framed photograph of the unfortunate Mrs. Hathaway and two sparkling children. A placard or poster, done in the style of Toulouse Lautrec, its legend: "Be like Dad, keep mum." A handsome mirror, framed in modernistic plastic (for Hathaway to admire himself in, of course). A half-open door leads to another door which leads, I know perfectly well, to a bedroom. At last I return to Hathaway. Gondzik is seated on a smaller chair, swivelling from side to side, spectacles gleaming.

"Well, then," Hathaway says, and sighs, sips his drink, lights a small cigar. "You'll be wondering why we sent for you."

I make some interested sound. He decides to get to the point, looking at me keenly with blue eyes, man to man instead of man to woman. "We would like you to come and work with us." He observes my reaction. So does Gondzik. I am careful not to react.

"What would you want me to do?"

He leans back, serious but tender. "You understand, of course, that it is vital that the security of this place should not only be kept intact. It must be strengthened. By your own work, since you returned from the West Wing—which unfortunately is outside our jurisdiction—you have shown how keenly you appreciate this fact. Only a woman, and only—now I see you I can, of course, appreciate this—yourself could have infiltrated into that subversive group, and used the methods that you did to make them play into our hands. It must have been unpleasant for you. Let's not mince words. I have no time for faggots. But the time has unfortunately come when we have to treat them very carefully, very carefully indeed. Just the other day I told Gondzik—you remember, Gondzik?—that the word 'faggot' must no longer be used on these premises. I am talking to you, of course, in confidence."

"Of course," I say. I don't know why, since I have noticed the tapes in the machines in the other office smoothly turning.

"This particular group was all the more dangerous for

being intelligent. Thanks to you, we have managed to deal with that. I'm merely sketching the scene for you, you understand. Putting you in the picture." He also seems to put this phrase in quotes, as though it were a snatch of French or Latin. I smile, to show I understand.

"So. To get to the point, since I'm sure you'll have no patience with me if I'm long-winded." A ravishing smile. There are so many smiles, followed by so much gravity. "In order to keep our security intact, we have certain simple devices, perfectly innocent of course, but necessary."

I hear myself say, "The lamps. The light switches."

"Precisely." Oh, he is pleased with me. "Of course all of you there are absolutely free. This is a free place. Everyone is equal. We call each other by first names, don't we, Basil? We all muck in together for the common good. No one would dream of putting any obvious pressure . . . on minorities. . . ."

"Of course," she says impatiently. "I understand."

Hathaway looks at me sharply for a moment. Apparently what he sees leads him to even deeper confidence.

"Good." He leans back, his arm stretched forward, tenderly brooding over the long ash of his cigar before it drops into the ashtray. He is now comrade to comrade. "Now as you may have heard, we are having a certain amount of trouble with our security. Things have got out of hand. In the first instance, the Board requested to see our tapes. Tapes, of course you appreciate, of the greatest . . ."

"Confidence," she supplies.

"Precisely." Leaning forward again, elbows on desk, he glances at Gondzik and smiles, as though to keep Gondzik going. "We dealt with that one. We insisted on—"

"Executive privilege."

But she is going too fast for him. A comrade she may be, but still a woman. He is faintly displeased. Gondzik almost imperceptibly shakes his head.

"I'm sorry," I say. "Please go on."

"They were stumped for a while. We were pretty sure

they couldn't get round executive privilege." The way he says the words, they sound like the name of an ex-Playmate, a thoroughly good sort. "Then some idiot spent a couple of days in the library and came up with a loophole. The tapes were inaccessible, you understand. But transcripts of the tapes, in his opinion, were not."

I am incredulous. She is impressed. Hathaway sighs deeply, as though the whole thing is too idiotic. Which (I think) it is.

"We agreed, therefore, to submit transcripts of the tapes." It is an honest sacrifice, anything for a bit of peace. "We would like you to transcribe those tapes. Clearly, honestly, with the interests of our security—your security —the security of all your friends over there—at heart."

Hathaway has finished, he has said his piece. Giving us time to consider, he snaps his fingers towards Gondzik. "Gondzik, drinks."

The whole thing is absurd. Does he really believe those tapes will be honestly transcribed? Of course not. That's why he asked me here, that's where he made his mistake. He's not only asking me to be a spy, he's asking me to be a dishonest spy. Oh repulsive Hathaway, who killed my dog and had me trapped by the gardener and encouraged all my vices for his own ends. I am sick with disgust and anger.

"I'd be glad to help you," she says. "When would you like me to start?"

Hathaway laughs merrily, disclosing a treasure of teeth.

"But, sweetheart, you haven't said a thing about money!"

"Money?" I ask, startled.

"Shall we say . . . a thousand a week? With all your expenses, of course."

"Well," she says, a shrewd glint in her eye, "I'm used to fifteen hundred, but of course if it's an emergency . . ."

"Twelve-fifty."

She shrugs her shoulders as though slipping off lacy shoulder straps, smiles and nods. I am stunned, bewildered, the idiot trailing along far in the rear. Gondzik is smiling, having won his hunch against considerable odds. What am I to do with the money? What is it for? What kind of money?

"But what shall I do with it?" I ask. "I mean, there's nothing . . ."

Hathaway glances at Gondzik: he can take this over.

"If you like," Gondzik says, "we put into the company for you, as an investment of course. We pay eight per cent and you can withdraw it at any time. What most of our employees do is to invest, say, two thirds of their salary against their . . . well, retirement, you might say. The rest you can spend in the Committee Store." He smiles, that pretty clearing in the grizzle. "It sells everything from St. Laurent to soap, you'll have a ball."

"And accommodation?" she asks, slurring the word a little, looking at Hathaway.

"For the moment, you'll stay where you are. Keep your eyes open, of course."

"Ear to the ground?" I ask faintly.

They both laugh. It seems that of the two of us, she and I, I have the better sense of humour.

"Well, then," Hathaway says. "How about tomorrow?"

"All right."

"About nine-thirty?"

"How shall I know," I ask, "when it's nine-thirty?"

"Christ, I almost forgot." He slides open a drawer in his desk, brings out a slim oblong box, hands it to us with extravagant gallantry over the desk. "For you."

It is a dainty watch; the entire works, I think, are made of diamonds. I would throw it in the trash can, along with the other litter from Christmas crackers. She gasps with wonder, slips it over her wrist, actually extends her arm to see it better, breathing gratitude and admiration. "Oh, but it's so pretty!" she sighs, "so cute!" and suchlike inanities, until I wonder whether she's lost her senses. Hathaway is delighted. I can tell that he is planning all manner of treats when he's told the secretary she can go home and visit her aged mother, or baby-sit for her plain girl friend.

"Don't flash it around," Gondzik says. He sounds, I think, a little acid. "You know the rules."

I look at him with contempt and loathing. Imagine confusing him with . . . but that's so long ago, I don't know his name any more. I see Mrs. April sitting in my room in the West Wing, pressing her hands together, looking down, looking up: the experience itself is . . . indelible. A moment's grief tornades through my heart, which is waiting inside me: it sweeps through as a tempestuous but tearless storm, leaving my heart dry and aching. I have nothing to say. She, the other, pushes the watch a little up her forearm, so that it is hidden by the cotton sleeve.

"Would it be terrible," she murmurs, "if I asked for just a tiny advance . . . I haven't a thing to wear. . . ."

Hathaway summons Gondzik with a backward jerk of his head. Gondzik goes to the neo-Lautrec poster, folds it back, turns the dials of a safe, opens it, looks sourly over his shoulder. "How much?"

"A thousand?" Hathaway asks.

"Twelve-fifty," she says, "would be better."

Not having a purse, she holds the bundle of notes in my hand, where they stick together, become soggy. Hathaway gets up, benign but quietly suggestive. He walks round the desk. I get up. He looks into everyone's eyes, knowing this to be the best policy.

"We're so glad," he says, "to have you with us. The Director will be overjoyed. . . ."

"He has seen me," I say, meaning that on the two previous occasions the Director was not overjoyed.

"The circumstances were a little . . . unfortunate." The smile again, the searching, yearning eyes. "After all, you're a . . . new woman."

"Yes," she whispers. "I really do feel . . . reborn. I really do."

I don't know why I stand there so passive, being gazed at. Perhaps I'm preserving myself so that when this is over (and it will, like everything else, be over) I shall still exist. I know that my eyes are troubled, but that her lashes are thick and long, curtaining my eyes.

"We'll have . . . lunch," he says. "Very soon. And talk about everything."

He stands there, looking after us as Gondzik leads us away. My back creeps with horrible anticipation: horrible, and yet it's so long since the West Wing, so long since I was treated as a woman, a pretty thing, an object of desire, an acquisition. My back seems to move towards him, not away.

"Well," Gondzik snaps, "you certainly did all right with Hathaway. Want to go shopping?"

The Committee Store is enormous, department after department full of spoils. I drag behind, wondering why they have all this for so few customers, why the prices are so outrageous, why I'm not in the least interested in tweed and cashmere and underwear, expensive bags and shoes and (my God, I haven't seen them since . . . I'm sure the old woman doesn't wear them) gloves. Gondzik, however, shows extraordinary interest, sweeping her from counter to counter, sitting and waiting while she tries things on and emerges like a butterfly from the fitting room, twisting and turning for his approval. It will all be delivered, of course. I shall have to move the dressing table from in front of my cupboard door. My cupboard will be crammed. Thank God there are four dressing tables, she'll need at least three of them. I have given Gondzik the handful of notes, but he charges it all to the Committee.

"But," I protest weakly, "he gave me the money . . ."

He looks at me with mock despair. "You'll learn, baby, you'll learn."

I look blank. I feel blank. He grins. "Remember the tennis courts. . . . ?"

She giggles. "Oh. Of course."

But back in the mansion, climbing the familiar stairs (the drip-drip of the fountain the only sound at this time of day, as at night), I find I'm alone again. Presumably she's gone off somewhere with Gondzik, perhaps up to the white chapel to pray. I let myself into my room and make for the rocking chair. When Mavis cleans the room (which she now does more often than necessary, because she loves to chatter), she always turns the rocking chair to face the room, being sociable. I always turn it back again, to look out of the window. Having done this, I sit, feet propped on the sill. The temperature outside Hathaway's air-conditioned office is in the high nineties, so someone said. My drawn blinds let in slits of sunlight, I can't look out of the window, I look at the still blind on which I have tied the shred, the remnant of a balloon from another age.

18

I wait, but she doesn't appear before breakfast, she doesn't appear at breakfast. I sit with Rowena and the reformed Adam. I haven't looked around me for some time, being preoccupied with other things, and am shocked to find how depressed and lifeless Rowena has become. Her cropped hair, at first little more than bristle, has grown dully over her ears; her sad, accusing eyes are burned into the pallid face; her body seems hardly able to support the weight of her eternal cover-up, the shapeless shroud she wears from morning till night. Even now he is normalised, Adam obviously hates suffering of this kind. He keeps his eyes firmly on his scrambled eggs until he has finished them, then on his coffee until he has finished that.

"Are you all right?" I ask her softly, a foolish question since she is so obviously dying.

She nods, shrinking into herself.

"Is there anything . . . I can do?"

She looks up at me, attempts to smile, to make a sad joke of it. "I guess I miss Simon."

"Simon?"

"Of course you were away most of the time. Simon. I miss him."

"Oh. I see."

There's nothing more to say. I take my cup, glass and plate into the kitchen (winked at by Mavis) and go upstairs. The room is still empty, except for a huge pile of packages on what might be called the day-bed. I pace up and down in bare feet, sit in a number of chairs. But Simon (and isn't even the name forbidden?) was mine. Simon lived in a room in the West Wing. Simon went away and would be happy in a couple of days and is staying with his peers. What peers? Where? How can Rowena possibly miss Simon? How did Rowena even know Simon? You mean that he knew other people here? He wasn't just brought here for my benefit? You mean that Simon—beyond my generous fantasies, my tolerant and maternal fantasies—had *a life of his own?*

I force myself to consider Rowena. Though destroyed, she is quite young; or was quite young. I think of Rowena daily diminishing in Simon's absence, while we were telling stories to each other, while we were celebrating, while he was sauntering into my womb (just thought I'd take a look at the old place), while I explored his bones as though he were a small cathedral made out of ivory. I am burning inside, suddenly knowing that I have often burned so, and often in dreams. Rowena?

At the height of my bewilderment and passion (of course reason is there too, but what it says is dreary, it can't gain my attention), she is tearing open the packages with a kind of cold severity, choosing this and that, discarding the rest for Mavis to put away. She glances at her exquisite watch, carefully nestling inside her elbow; she puts on panties and a brassiere, not seeming to find this restricting; she stands at one of the dressing tables and deftly, hardly looking in the mirror, enhances her face; she pulls on tights, gathering each leg in her hand, smoothing them up from the toe over the knee, wriggling a little to settle them over her hips; she fastens a skirt, swivels it round, the placket at the back; she buttons three buttons of a nine-buttoned sweater; she brushes

165

her hair, leaning her head first this way, then that. She seems angry, like someone going out to battle.

However, unwillingly, I still have to go with her; after all, we share the same body so far. She runs briskly down the stairs, good handbag swinging from her shoulder and out (I am totally amazed) through the front door. I have never been through the front door. She strides (though the strides are short and ladylike) down a driveway, suddenly turns into a subsidiary road which, tarmaced, goes straight through the woods. She is muttering to herself now she is out of any possible sight. I know what she is saying. It is the first time we are almost friendly. "Rowena, for God's sake . . . no, it's not true . . . it's perfectly obvious . . . he was sly, that's what it was, sly . . . but come on, I was there forever before he came, he had to do something . . . how dare she miss him, how dare *she* miss him . . . I'll kill her . . . I'll comfort her." My love (I say). *My* boy friend (she says). We march on, wanting to stone Rowena with pine cones.

Now we are crossing the flower garden. Nobody there. I look up, to see if I can spot the window of my room in the West Wing. All the blinds are drawn, all the windows identical. We take to the straight grass path. The grass is burned, lacking rain, and her heels don't sink into the ground. The petunias are shrivelled, the box hedges parched, a few roses hang withered heads from the pergolas, hanged roses. I am occupied, overwhelmed, with a longing to see the old woman again. She, more practical, twists off a few dead heads on her way. We go on and on (I thought Gondzik said this was a short cut) until at last, in the far distance, I see the stone seat crusted with bird lime. It is empty. You aren't sitting there like a judge, a doorman, a janitor, an executioner. We take a left, as Gondzik instructed, by the stone seat. We are at the side door of the office. We go in (deferentially saluted), plunging into the ice-cold air with a gasp.

Up in the elevator (we shall get used to this, never allowing it to go farther), a brief knock on Room 31, enter before the secretary flutes come in. The secretary is pleased to see her, offers coffee from a chromium machine, shows her through Hathaway's office (which is empty) to the room where the still tapes (no, one is steadily turning) wait behind transparent doors. There is a desk, a lamp, a typewriter, sharpened pencils, paper of all sizes, a dictionary and a Roget (crime, guilt 947; criminal, vicious 945; culprit, 949; malefactor 975) and a comfortable chair. The tapes, she takes in at a glance, are neatly filed, the padlocks on the cases already opened.

"I'll show you how it works," the secretary says.

"I know," she says, and hangs her handbag on a hook.

"Mr. Hathaway said that you'll find some of them a little . . . incoherent." She is well educated, this secretary, a good school, excellent college degree, plenty of experience. "But that he leaves it to you to make them—"

"Clearer."

"More . . . clear."

"All right. I'll begin."

"If there's anything you want," the secretary says, and giggles once, "just holler."

We are left alone with the tapes. As she takes the first one out of the file, briefly examines its front and its flip side, fits it into the machine, I passionately hope that the huge Brandenburg will burst into the room, the office, sweep away the entire building. Instead of this there is crackling, breathing.

"You have been here in the winter. You have . . . it was cold, very cold, your feet froze to the ground! . . . The lake was frozen, you walked across it, she was skating cutting figures of eight, she was eight, wasn't she—"

"Her little skirt like daisy petals flung out from a yellow stem, she loves me, loves me not—"

"You plucked them, leaving her shivering."

"GODDAMN YOU!"

She presses some button, the tape stops, she settles herself in her chair, adjusts the lamp. Even I am intrigued, as though looking through an old photograph album, amused and curious. She doesn't look amused. She fixes her earphones, presses another button and sits stony-faced, occasionally scribbling something in neat handwriting.

GONDZIK   I don't remember. I experience.

MYSELF   My God, you're just like all the others! What's the matter with you in this place? Keep off the grass, don't pee in stationary trains, Walk, Don't Walk, No Smoking. What d'you *mean* you don't remember, you just experience? It's a . . . slogan, isn't it, something you learned off pat. I know what you think you are, you think you're a revolutionary, don't you? Jesus Christ, you don't know what revolution *is!* I don't either, but then I don't pretend to, I just want to be free to . . . well, walk on the grass, pee when I feel like it, cross streets when it's obviously safe, I want to tell *myself* when it's dangerous to smoke. That's what it's like where I come from, wherever it is, but here your so-called freedom's like a bloody nursery! You don't begin to know what it is, freedom! . . . I've seen you when you think I'm going to break a rule, when anyone's going to break a rule, you go quite sick with terror, you really look quite *sick* at the idea that someone might behave unsuitably, particularly if it involves you! I mean, Gondzik is the strong one, the right one, the rich one, the one who gets his bed made every day because he bribes the bloody workers! You're safe, aren't you, because you're so fucking *smart,* you know all the names for everything, you can kill other people and play awful games with other people, but if anyone tries to do the same to you, sitting up here monarch of all you survey with all that sex boiling round in your head and no way out for it! If anyone tries to do the same to you . . . But of course they don't. They never will, will they? And you're so sweet at heart, sweetheart. You never did anything horrible to a little girl on the pond, did you? You didn't tear off her skirt like daisy petals or whatever awful phrase it was? You didn't set fire to the bloody Reichstag or shoot those students or drop a single tiny atom of a bomb or gas, gas a single person of your own race, did you? No, you're just a scribe, a Pharisee! You play innocent, you've got the Right Ideas, you don't remember, you only experience, and you sit there mumbling that like the Talmud while just at the bottom of your garden the cattle trucks are rattling by, do you know that? The *cattle trucks!* . . . Okay. So you're laughing. Of course, you have to. That's one of the most tedious things about you, the ghastly noise of it, ha ha ha if anyone tells you the truth. It's *your* job to tell the truth. No one else knows it, of course, It's your private possession. And you trick it out to look like fire and brimstone, your truth is so *significant*, not like anyone else's. Go on! *Laugh* Louder! Louder! You're a liar, Gondzik, but you think that the beauty of it is that no one else knows! You're a bully, but it's *you* who do the sissy-kissing, you're the teacher's pet, keeping everyone quiet with your incessant yatter, beating them down if they even take a breath, giving your awful bounty to poor simple girls who'd be grateful for a crust of bread, an old grapestalk! You don't want to *change* what you call the system! You just want to suck its blood and pretend it's soda pop, one of those filthy drinks you drink, baby drinks. That's what keeps you alive, the system! . . . I'm so delighted to be entertaining you! God, that's what I'm for, isn't it? To entertain Gondzik? You'd be *lost* without the system! You wouldn't have any father or mother or brothers or sisters or simple girls or girls to adore you or heroes to wipe your feet on! You'd be abandoned, Gondzik! You'd be thrown away, like an old Gauleiter who's no use any more! You think you could ever learn to be humble without resenting it? Just the word "humble" makes you laugh, doesn't it? There's no such thing as humility in your book, that's in the other book, the later one written by Matthew, Mark, Luke and John, remember? It's a strength, not a weakness,

but you'd never learn that, would you, not on your life!
And you know it's possible to be proud without being
cruel, possible to love your enemies with righteous in-
dignation? You'll rupture yourself if you laugh so much.
. . . Tyrants are the weaklings, you fool! Tyrants like
you, barking and braying and forming people up in
straight lines, in straight pigeon-holes, in straight li-
braries with straight censors, in straight speeches that
go on and on and on and on without making the slightest human sense. . . . (*The sound of weeping super-
imposed on laughter.*) Damn you and your rules for
freedom and your silly tricks with time and your cheating, cheating. . . . Damn you!
(*There is a long silence.*)

GONDZIK There's no point in being here if you don't go
along with it, obey the rules as you say. It's one of the
few situations which one can quite validly call a waste
of time. Why don't you leave?

At the end of this scene, which I listen to with relish, she
with a face like stone, there is a click, a moment's silence.
Then Gondzik's voice: "she's hopelessly misguided, of
course, but shows spirit. I calmed her down. It will be interesting to note her progress from now on."

❋ ❋ ❋

There are a surprising number of tapes of people making
love, men and women, men, women. On the whole they
seem to me rather uninteresting and completely unsubver-
sive, but she stabs the paper with her pointed pencil, stopping and starting again and stopping as though she were
writing a sex manual. Leonora and Dominic. Elizabeth and
Gondzik (his voice is unmistakeable, but it was, as he points
out, for her own good). Adam, Bill, Hugh and their satel-
lites, in various combinations; the blonde (and among
others Gondzik again, I'm sure of it) who really does give
a good performance—(after these, Gondzik suggesting that
with certain minor alterations, they could be sold at considerable profit). Leonora and . . . Rowena? Rowena and

Hermann, perhaps, the forgotten anthropologist. I'm astonished by the quantity and variety of activity, when, apart from the battalion, I had thought them all so passive. Myself and George (I am shocked, but for once she smiles). Myself and the weeping man, the action drowned by those tearing sobs. Often she pauses, adjusts her earphones as though they were a hearing aid, gives her head a sharp shake to clear it, listens intently over and over to the same sounds, apparently having difficulty in identifying a voice.

ROWENA (*Laughing, sighing*) Don't go away . . . come here . . . that's right . . . I love you . . . I said "love", l-o-v-e. It's quite respectable, you know . . . love is. Don't look so shocked. . . . Do you love me?

Maybe she was murmuring into her mirror, for there's no reply beyond protesting bedsprings. In this way I learn a great deal about the people in the place, their hopes and disappointments, their ability to feel. Of course I already know that Gondzik had set up the affair with George, and this will presumably be to his credit; but for the rest, I can't believe there is anything damaging to the office, politics having very little place in encounters of this sort.

* * *

UNIDENTIFIABLE VOICE What's the matter?

ROWENA Nothing.

VOICE Yes, there is. What is it?

ROWENA Nothing.

VOICE Look, don't be silly. . . . That's better.

Long pause.

VOICE Now. What's the matter?

ROWENA I'm . . . frightened.

VOICE What of?

ROWENA Nothing.

A deep sigh.

VOICE Well. If you won't tell me, I can't help you. Can I?

ROWENA I'm pregnant.

Pause.

      VOICE   Oh God.

Long pause.

      ROWENA What shall I do?

      VOICE   I don't know. (*Pause*) I don't know, I don't know, I don't know.

      ROWENA I knew you wouldn't know.

      VOICE   Jesus, I don't know! (*Pause*) How long?

      ROWENA You know I can't tell how long. A long time.

      VOICE   Why didn't you tell me before, for God's sake?

      ROWENA You wouldn't have known then, would you? I mean what to do. There wasn't any point. I talked to Elizabeth and Leonora.

      VOICE   What did they say?

      ROWENA They didn't know.

Long pause.

      VOICE   It doesn't show. I suppose that's why you keep that thing on all the time.

      ROWENA Yes. (*Pause*) Don't be angry.

      VOICE   I'm not angry, I'm *not* angry. . . . Oh God, I'm sorry.

      ROWENA Now you're crying.

Long pause. The voice pulls itself together.

      VOICE   Well. What shall we do? Have you tried . . . hot baths and things?

      ROWENA I've tried hot baths. Do you think that woman would know? The one who's by herself all the time? She looks . . . as though she might know.

      VOICE   I think she's away somewhere. I haven't seen her since the play.

      ROWENA Then what shall we do?

      VOICE   I don't know.

The tape whirs and clicks to a stop. Of course I am horrified. What was I doing—putting the house in order? Hathaway, scented even from here, puts his head round the door.

"Good morning, sweetheart. You look sensational today. How's it going?"

"Fine," she answers, fluttering a little.

"Interesting?"

"Oh, very."

"I'll look forward to your report. I'm tied up for lunch, unfortunately. How about a quick drink at the end of the day?"

When the shadows lengthen and the evening comes. "Lovely," she says.

Hathaway disappears. She fits another tape into the machine, fiddles with the earphones, poises the pencil, frowning with concentration.

* * *

ROWENA I really didn't want to bother you, but you seem so . . . well, I mean, as though you might know.

VOICE That's perfectly all right, sweetie. Poor little thing. I tell you what, I'll talk it over with the woman when she comes back. The one who's always at the pool. We'll think of something. Never fear. What a ghastly bore it must be.

Is it Adam, Hugh or Bill? Cocking our head, we try to hear the finer nuances. Adam, we decide.

ROWENA There's just no one I can . . . well, ask. I never see him now. I mean, only at breakfast, and then he doesn't speak much. Well, you can't say anything at breakfast, can you?

ADAM Now dry those pretty little eyes. Women crying does something quite terrible to me. I want to slice their heads off. Do you know where he goes?

ROWENA No. He won't tell me. He just doesn't care.

ADAM Of course he cares. He's probably just scared out of his tiny little wits. Now are you going to be a good girl and leave it to Uncle Adam?

ROWENA   Yes. Yes, all right. Thank you.
A click, a scrape, new voices.

* * *

HUGH/BILL   But how absurd!

BILL/HUGH   I always did think she was a stupid little slut.

ADAM   But what the hell am *I* supposed to do? You think a corkscrew might serve?

HUGH/BILL   Not at this juncture, I'm sure. My mother is a mine of information on these subjects.

ADAM   But your mother isn't here, is she? We'll have to think of something. At least she wears that djellabah all the time.

BILL/HUGH   Ah, Tunis . . .

ADAM   Anyway, the woman will probably know. She looks just the sort.

HUGH/BILL   Surely we can think of something *amusing* to do? I mean, it's all so dreary. We could liven it up a bit.

I am feeling sick. In spite of the air conditioning, the office seems stifling. My heart is knocking, trying to give me some message; anxiety makes me want to clench my hands, but they are busy writing. Let me out, let me out. But no, imprisoned in this now unfamiliar body, I'm forced to listen.

* * *

ROWENA   I'm so sorry to bother you. . . . Did you manage to talk to her?

ADAM   Who?

ROWENA   That woman. She's back. And I've seen her going to the pool.

ADAM   I saw *you* talking to her the other day. Didn't you say anything?

ROWENA   I couldn't. I think we bore her. Somehow I can't.

ADAM   And where's the proud father? Hopped it, I suppose?

ROWENA   I think they sent him away. I don't know why.

ADAM   For pity's sake, dear, do stop crying. I'll talk to her today. I promise.
Silence. The sound of sobbing.

*   *   *

ROWENA   I'm so sorry to bother you again. . . . Have you talked to her?

ADAM   Who? Oh . . . yes. Yes, of course. She said . . . it's much too late to do anything about it, but she'll talk to Gondzik. She has influence with Gondzik for some reason, such a brute. She says . . . you'll have to grin and bear it, dear, Gondzik may be able to arrange something.

ROWENA   But I don't *want* it!

ADAM   Silly girl. You should have thought of that before, shouldn't you.
Silence.

*   *   *

LEONORA/ELIZABETH   Christ! Is that *it?*

ROWENA   Yes.

ELIZABETH/LEONORA   Is it alive?

ROWENA   Yes.

ELIZABETH/LEONORA   It's terribly small, isn't it?

ROWENA   Yes.

LEONORA/ELIZABETH   What happened?

ROWENA   Well . . . the pains began. I didn't know what to do. I went out somewhere, I don't know, into the woods somewhere. I could hear them . . . playing by the pool. So I went further, I mean very far. I sat down under a tree. It was funny, because there was a squirrel, it kept running up to me, it couldn't . . . do anything. Then . . . the pains got worse. So I lay down. Then I remembered that someone told me you should . . . you know . . . squat down, that's what

175

savages do. But I couldn't get up very well, though I tried. Then an old woman came.

ELIZABETH/LEONORA   What old woman? Who?

ROWENA   I don't know. She just came with her little chair, you know, one of those folding chairs? And she sat by me and she said, "Hold my hand". So I did, and after a bit . . . I don't know, I'm afraid I hurt her hand. But she told me what to do and she kept saying that's good, that's good, good girl, that's good.

LEONORA/ELIZABETH   What was good?

ROWENA   And I bit her hand. It was very old, quite brown, you know, with veins . . . veins. And then it was terrible. And then it was born.

A long silence.

ELIZABETH/LEONORA   My God.

LEONORA/ELIZABETH   Then what happened?

ROWENA   She had a pair of . . . secateurs. She cut it off. She made it very neat, I think. She said the afterbirth . . . the placenta? . . . had come away with the baby. So she wiped the baby, I think with her dress, and wrapped it in her shawl. Then she looked at me for a long time. She was crying. Then she went away.

Silence. Long silence.

* * *

HUGH/BILL   What an exquisite idea! What genius!

BILL/HUGH   Just imagine her face when she finds it!

ADAM   I still think we should get her to do it. I mean . . . it's more of a woman's job, really.

HUGH/BILL   But then it wouldn't be a surprise! We want it to be a surprise!

BILL/HUGH   A treat.

HUGH/BILL   She'll laugh like anything.

ADAM   I'm not sure. Maybe it'll make her all dingy and glum again.

BILL/HUGH   Why should it? It's not her brat, after all. Oh come on, Adam . . . go and get the thing.

ADAM I'd much rather we asked her. I don't even know how to . . . carry it.

HUGH/BILL But you must have played with dolls, sweetie. When you were a child.

BILL/HUGH Whenever that was.

HUGH/BILL Adam's chicken! Adam's chicken!

ADAM Oh, all right. Give me some of that, you bastards.

BILL/HUGH That, my love, is what's known as Dutch courage.

Silence.

* * *

ADAM I've come to get it. Where is it?

ROWENA Here it is.

ADAM Jesus Christ. Isn't it very . . . small?

ROWENA Yes.

ADAM Is it . . . a boy or a girl?

ROWENA A girl.

ADAM Thank God for that. I don't need this old shawl. I'll put it under my shirt, okay?

ROWENA I'm . . . sorry.

ADAM Not to worry, baby. Here's some candy, it'll make you feel a lot better.

ROWENA Thank you.

ADAM New life, yes? Make yourself pretty? It won't cry, will it?

ROWENA She's too small to cry.

ADAM Right, then. You just lie there and think beautiful thoughts.

ROWENA Thank you.

* * *

If there was any more, I didn't hear any more. In the evening, she probably had a drink with Hathaway. I didn't notice. As far as I know, I stayed where I was, staring at the silent tapes.

19

Sometimes, in the mornings when she's getting to go to work, we talk.

"But I don't understand. Adam never said anything to me. He never asked me."

"Well. There it is. What would you have done, anyway?"

"I don't know. We could have kept it."

"Don't be ridiculous."

"But why do they think I planned it? Why do they think I was working for them?"

"You weren't. I was. I'm having my hair done this afternoon."

"But how could you be . . . when I . . . ?"

"Why not just accept it? Let them think what they like? We're onto a good thing, after all."

"We're not! It's evil! What are you going to do next?"

"I don't know. God, I'll be glad to get my hair done. I think it's time we had a show-down of some sort. You know those tapes of Mavis, for instance?"

"No!"

"Such a silly woman, always chattering, terribly indiscreet." She fixes her eyelashes as easily as sticking on stamps. "And then, there's Gondzik . . ."

"But Gondzik works for them!"

"I know." She smiles, dreamily. "That's the beauty of it."

"What you're writing down—it has nothing to do with the tapes, nothing!"

"I always wanted to be a writer. Such fun. Just a tiny basis of truth and presto"—she turns, radiant—"a star is born!"

"Can't I kill you?"

"I shouldn't think so. When this is over, I'll be leaving anyway."

"Where to?"

"I don't know." She shrugs, dusts one shoulder. "To make my fortune?"

I am always baffled. I always lumber about the room, heavily, lamenting. I bore her, I know that.

"But how can you work for them? They're criminals!"

She fixes me with calm eyes, the same colour as my own. "I'm continually surprised by what appears to be your new-found sense of morality. Forgive me, but . . . you never seemed very concerned with such things. I think you believed in convenience, something like that. All this seems to bring it out. I must say, your highly emotional idealism makes it difficult to reason with you, but they always say converts are the worst. You must admit that anyone who behaves as you have, jumping in and out of bed with all and sundry—some of them married men—not to mention baby-snatching—and proving yourself quite incapable of tidying and cleaning a simple house . . . well, perhaps you're not the best spokeswoman for ethics. Of course all that's easy to forget with your modern rationalisation. So why don't you allow the rationalisations in the office, where they're merely doing things—just as you did—for personal gain, or maybe just for the challenge? Or even for some insane belief in our security? I mean, is it simply a matter of scope, who's affected? Or aren't you accountable for your acts? Do you want honest men—and women, of course—over there, running things, so that you can be free to . . . well, commit your own little moral crimes in safety? . . . No, wait a minute. It's so easy for us to rationalise our own indulgences and immoral acts—why do we expect the administration to be above such things? Why be so shocked when you discover that some of them, too, are just as humanly frail and faulted? I believe you thought something along these lines when you first came here. I don't know what's happened to make you change your mind. It's a grave pity."

"I was innocent," I say, "then."

"Indeed you were. I'd advise you to . . . recapture your innocence."

"You know I can't do that."

"Invent it, then."

"I can't do that, either. Besides, I'm right."

"You're hopelessly wrong."

"Are you going to . . . have me up? Try me?"

"Unfortunately, I can't." She does have a pretty smile, mischievous and yet open. "United, we stand. Divided, for the time being at any rate, we fall. Well, are you ready?"

So off we go. I'm beginning to feel like Caliban tagging along behind Ariel. The stone bench is always empty. I haven't dreamed about you, or at least remembered my dreams, for aeons. Perhaps I miss them. They were remarkably real illusions, full of natural incident and feeling. Now she has taken over, all charm and confidence, the right word for every occasion, I have no escape except into my childhood, and that place—so rich, I know, if you want richness—is beginning to bore and disappoint me. The old woman tends to other women, nurses their children. The pinewoods are merely pinewoods. I feel I am almost back to the numb time, when things were things, names were names, I was no one.

We continue to transcribe the tapes. Hathaway is delighted. They have little cocktail parties now, after work, just the two of them. She asks me to go with her, but I won't, I block my ears, running off into whatever hole or cranny I can find for privacy, watching two kittens (Troilus and Pushkin?) unravelling wool, searching the shelves of supermarkets, posting letters in red letter boxes, wondering where my next meal is coming from. There's little comfort or entertainment in this, and I suppose I sometimes feel envious of her, sparkling away with Hathaway's hand creeping up her thigh. The days I spent in the rocking chair were best, rocking and watching my world go by. Now I am dragged out every day by this detestable wardress, I don't know what to do with myself. I accuse myself of inexcusable passivity. Why don't I just wreck the tapes while she's sipping her icy drinks, squealing appreciation at Hathaway's wit? Why do I just sit here? I have nothing to lose. They couldn't execute me, not without damaging her strong neck. But they might do that. I can't be responsible for another's death. Only my own. So the dull thoughts, confused with saucers of milk and instant coffee and postage stamps, go plodding through my mind and out the other side and round again.

One evening—a little tipsy, I think—she is full of excitment. She won't tell me why; or else she tells me, but I refuse to listen. The next morning we don't go into the tape room, but remain in Hathaway's office. Chairs have been placed in a semi-circle, Hathaway's desk at the apex. There is one chair in the centre of the semi-circle. We sit close to Hathaway's desk, at a small table equipped with writing materials, a carafe of water and a glass.

People begin to arrive, strangers, administrators I presume. They are mostly men of Hathaway's vintage, kept trim by badminton and tennis, well massaged and manicured. The few women wear jersey suits with large, expensive brooches, it is obvious that they constantly attend their hairdressers and, like the men, keep themselves lithe and healthy. When Hathaway enters, even more tanned and affable than usual, they tease him with small, personal jokes, demonstrating their familiarity with the great. He takes this with huge good humour, settles himself in his chair, prepares to make a speech of some sort. The door of our office is shut, but I know that she has switched on the tape machines. The secretary, who has grown flustered and a little wild of late, arrives in a pretty turmoil murmuring that she overslept. Hathaway looks at her coldly. She settles herself in her place, all legs and, for once, improperly distributed hair. Hathaway resumes his preparations for a speech.

It is, of course, about security and insecurity. I barely listen. There is something about the fall of a sparrow, which I don't understand anyway. Now he is talking about ants undermining great cities, quite poetical this morning. I think she must have written this for him. The audience looks awed. Hathaway has risen to new heights. He reads messages from the Director, who is indisposed. He calls us "My friends, my very dear friends." It must be moving, since the secretary is dabbing her eye. At last, Hathaway touches even himself; his voice grates with emotion; he lies back, hands hanging limp, delivered. The applause is of angels on Judgement Day, a kind of tinkling of ethereal hands, reverent congratulation.

The door bursts open, it seems, before the two guards can open it. Gondzik strides in, beard bristling, eyes whirling around behind the gold spectacles. He stands, pugnacious, ready to shoot a straight left to any whisper or shadow. The guards stand lumpishly behind him.

"Basil," Hathaway murmurs, reviving himself. "Dear boy . . . take a seat, do." With a courteous hand he indicates the centre chair. After some hesitation, bristling and glaring, Gondzik hauls the chair back with a scrape, turns it, straddles it, arms along the back. He gives me a hard look and I want to say that he has made rather a noble gesture, but keep silent.

"As you know, Basil," Hathaway says, leaning back at ease, "we have been transcribing these . . . wretched tapes so that the Board can see to its satisfaction exactly what we've been doing in the way of examining and strengthening our security measures. Naturally"—he laughs slightly, conceding this point—"you know all this as well as I do."

"But I don't know what the fucking hell this is all about," Gondzik snaps. "They've no right to come and arrest me in the gym."

"In the gym?" Hathaway is mildly shocked. "That's a shame. Let's get this over as quickly as possible, then." He holds out his hand, she fills it with a blue folder, he opens the blue folder and smooths it tenderly. "We have here a transcript of a conversation between yourself and my . . . new assistant. It is, of course, undated, but appears to have been the first of many such conversations."

"Well?" Gondzik barks. "We had frequent conversations."

"I know, I know . . . I'm not in very good voice today, I'm afraid, but perhaps if I read you the gist, shall we say, of some of your remarks on that occasion, you would be good enough to explain them?"

"Certainly." Gondzik is suddenly rather smug, he thinks he will do well in this kind of Dialogue.

"You begin"—Hathaway's finger traces the passage—"with a rather frank confession of a particularly nasty"—he looks up, beaming—"crime. We will, however, come back to that in due course. My assistant then . . . changes the conversation—obviously, I would think, distressed." She lowers her eyes with the slightest shudder. "She makes some ordinary, civil remark . . . let me see . . . yes: I'm so pleased to meet you. The sort of remark one might hear in any civilised, reasonably secure household." He looks up for confirmation; his civilised, reasonably secure audience nod their heads, smiling. "You then ask her—forgive me—if she remembers how you met. She replies quite correctly that she is concerned only with experience, and refuses to discuss memory . . . I'm sorry, Basil. Excuse me." He holds up his hand, stemming the bursting tide of Gondzik's denial. "You will have plenty of opportunity to speak later. This is simply an Investigation Committee. You must remember that you're among friends. Bear with me." He turns the page, frowning slightly. "You then launch into the most remarkable . . . tirade. You accuse my assistant, and through her our entire organisation—the organisation, Basil, that has cared for you and put you where you are today—of being lethargic and simple-minded. You say that we have no grasp of freedom." At this, his voice is so appalled that he almost chokes; she swiftly hands him a glass of water. "While appearing to recommend the most violent form of revolution, you simultaneously admit to setting fire to the Reichstag, shooting a number of harmless students, bombing innocent civilians and gassing a considerable number of . . . Jews. You even boast of these exploits, stating that you are smarter than anyone else, that you know all the names for everything, that you can kill with impunity—immunity?—that you can—and I quote—'play awful games with other people.'" This is too much. Hathaway sits back for a moment, gazing at Gondzik, who is temporarily stunned. "Basil, Basil . . ." Hathaway mourns, his head moving from side to side. The audience murmurs among itself. After allowing perhaps thirty seconds for their reaction to become law, Hathaway continues.

"Need I, need I, my friends, continue with this . . . puerile rubbish?" The question is rhetorical. "To give you some idea of what follows, our comrade, our ex-comrade here, insists that he wishes to suck our blood and pretend it's soda pop. He denies democracy, he denies the Gospels, he denies Our Lord himself. No. Wait. While raving like the lunatic which—I am sad to say—he must certainly be, he is laughing. It says here perfectly clearly, you can see it for yourselves: he is beside himself with *laughter*. Do I really have to say more?" Hathaway falls back, exhausted with emotion.

There is an appalled silence, all eyes on Gondzik. Who rises and comes towards me. Who stands over me.

"It's not true," he says.

She looks him calmly in the eye. "It is true. It is on the tape. A tape doesn't lie, Basil."

He whirls to Hathaway. "I demand to hear that tape!"

"I'm sorry, my dear fellow. The tapes are protected by executive privilege. This"—he taps the blue folder "—is a faithful transcript, the transcript that will be submitted to the Board."

Gondzik starts bawling that it's a lie, a lie, that he demands justice, a lawyer, a public apology. Hathaway waits

184

patiently, motioning the guards to step back as they move forward. He sighs, softly drumming a gold pen on the soft blotter. At last Gondzik, having run round in circles, collapses like a child playing musical chairs.

"That's better," Hathaway says. "I shall only touch briefly on the other, even more sordid, side of the case. You first admit to raping a little girl on a frozen . . . Cake?" He puzzles, peering. "I'm so sorry. Lake."

"She was my sister," Gondzik says stupidly.

Hathaway merely flicks him a glance. "You then get involved in infanticide."

"In what?"

"You persuade an unfortunate girl here—and God knows, we have every sympathy with the unmarried mother—to get rid of her child. You drown the infant. In our lily pond. Basil, what possessed you? Why didn't you come to me for help? We could have sent you to the West Wing, even though it is outside our jurisdiction. Basil—what have you done?"

Now why aren't I crying out? Why aren't I helping this poor blundering man, mopping and mowing his head like a stuck bull, blood about to pour from his nostrils? Because I have no voice. She has taken my voice. She sits there, looking smug and appalled, with my voice tucked inside her larynx. My pity for Gondzik—who did, after all, care for me according to his lights—is useless. If I smiled at him it would be an offence. How terrible it would be if it were the other one, the one I loved, the one I . . . But this diminishes Gondzik's real stature now, which God knows isn't all that high, he can't afford to be further belittled. My hatred for her, the woman who no longer even looks like me, is violent; but I have no weapons, seem powerless.

After a while Hathaway flips through Gondzik's minor crimes, such as assaulting the women, indulging in unnatural practices, trying to seduce even his assistant (murmurs of "shame!"), spying on the administration through binoculars, encouraging Revlon and other revolutionaries, and so on.

During this recital Gondzik revives a little. His wits are working. Unfortunately his wits are the latest, most highly perfected piece of machinery off the assembly line; but what is the machine's purpose, what can it produce? His wits race through their complicated routine, every part in mint condition, and produce nothing. His wits exist for their own sake, nothing more.

"I demand . . ." he says.

"Oh, Basil," Hathaway sighs. "Do stop demanding, it's so unsuitable. I think we should take a vote, but first, naturally, I will give you the alternatives. This transcript, together with many others, will be presented to the Board in the near future. The final decision is up to the Board. I am, of course, a member of the Board, but it will be a majority decision and who knows . . ." He smiles sadly, accepting the foibles of freedom. "In the meanwhile, as I see it, we as the Investigation Committee have two alternatives. Naturally I should be happy to hear any suggestions from you, since I may have overlooked other possible solutions." He glances up, is met by the composite devoted gaze. "In my opinion, we can do one of two things. Either we confine Basil here—under the most humane conditions, of course—until the Board meeting; or we arrange for him to be sent to the West Wing where—being outside our jurisdiction—he can be treated indefinitely, and may possibly become a responsible citizen. Do you want to know which of these alternatives I, personally, prefer?"

Of course they do. He clasps his hands, leaning forward on the desk, looking at Gondzik with fond, serious eyes.

"In my opinion—the West Wing. There are brilliant diagnosticians in the West Wing. The best in the world, I believe. It is my firm belief that the balance of Basil's mind has, of late, been disturbed. Basil is no criminal. He is an intelligent man. He needs help, rather than punishment. If we decide that he is fit to appear before the Board, there is no knowing what the decision will be. If we decide that he is deranged—which I firmly believe—and should be institutionalised, the Board will be relieved of a very arduous and unpleasant duty. The Boards has a great deal on its hands. Most of its members are exhausted. They have no rest, day or night. They have to return from their vacations, cancel their golf." He stops in the nick of time, knowing that more would be more than enough. He opens his hands, offering them the problem. "Friends, I suggest we vote."

The secretary gets up, hopelessly pushing at her hair. She distributes small pieces of white paper and sharpened pencils which for some inexplicable reason have the name Tawasentha printed on them in gold lettering. She gives one to Hathaway, and one to me—she, the assistant, is busy for the moment tipping tablets into the palm of her hand and giving them one by one to Hathaway to swill down with water. Before she can catch me, I write FREE GONDZIK and fold the paper. She sits, looks round for her paper, sees mine (I try to cover it with her hand), snatches it, reads it, crumples it with disgust and buries it in her brassiere. She has her own paper. She writes WEST WING in bold letters, folds it carefully, as though making a boat to sail in the bath.

"But you know," I whisper, "what they'll do to him in the West Wing."

"So much the better."

"And you know it's all lies, you know *I* said all that, you know it was me!"

She barely looks at me. "I thought you had lost your voice."

I take a breath. It's true. My voice has gone again, I can manage only an unintelligible croak. She hands me a throat lozenge, pink and encrusted with sugar. The secretary is collecting the votes in a kind of chalice. She goes into the outer office bearing the chalice with the distraught air of a divested virgin. A quiet murmur breaks out, Hathaway gets up and moves among his supporters, graceful and solemn. As he passes Gondzik, slumped on his chair, he presses his shoulder to give him courage.

The secretary comes back with an envelope, which she hands to Hathaway, which he opens. "The West Wing," he says; then, simply, gratefully to the audience, "Thank you."

Gondzik stands up. He looks at me directly. "Why did you do this?"

I make a huge effort, bursting my lungs. "I didn't. I'm sorry."

"She did nothing but transcribe the tapes," Hathaway says. "She shares, as we all do, my regret."

"Did I harm you?" Gondzik asks.

"Only a little."

"She makes light of it," Hathaway says. "She's a brave girl. We need more like her." There is a little patter of applause.

"What will they do to me there?"

"Change you. Unless you learn to pretend."

"We all have to learn to adjust," Hathaway says vaguely, passing his hand across his forehead. He is very tired.

"I don't understand," Gondzik says.

"No," I say. "That's the trouble."

"You will," Hathaway says. "In the end."

They lead Gondzik away. He doesn't look back. The secretary dispenses coffee in plastic cups.

* * *

Mavis is child's play. At first, when they bring her in, she thinks it's a surprise party. She is so pleased to see me: well, dear, what a lovely surprise and it's not even my birthday. At first she giggles and pats her hair, cheerfully admitting to stories of food shortages, rising prices, ever such lovely movies, lucky bets and family misfortunes. When it comes to the bit about them having him (Hathaway, as it happens) up in front of the Committee, her merry eyes suddenly freeze, she is all fear. Hathaway is not interested, he wants to get it over with. Mavis begins to cry, an unpleasant sight, all slobber and snot. She pleads with me to help her. I am dumb again. The vote is that she should be confined until the Board meeting, then tried. She is helped out, rather roughly, her pink shoulder straps slipped down over her buxom arms.

The Committee adjourns. Some people come up to congratulate Hathaway and his assistant. She murmurs that it was nothing, really nothing, she's so glad to have been helpful.

"She'll soon move on to higher things," Hathaway says proudly. "She's an artist, you know. A really free spirit. We'd be the last to try and clip her wings, wouldn't we? Before we know where we are, she'll be better off than any of us!"

"Invest in land," someone advises.

"I don't want much," she says modestly. "Just thirty acres."

That evening, for the first time, I go back alone, leaving her at the office. There are lights in the West Wing. Perhaps Gondzik's torture has already started. I have little hope of him learning to pretend. But if by any unlikely chance he does, perhaps someone will visit him. . . . Perhaps, in some curious way, he'll find grace.

I am so lonely. But that doesn't matter. I am so grieved, so sick. But that doesn't matter. Other people's pain knocks at the windows, cries at the locks, upstairs and downstairs, softly howling in the woods and gardens. I sit in the rocking chair, listening.

20

She is preparing to leave. She packs her new clothes in new suitcases. I sit and watch, getting in the way.

"It's quite maddening," she says. "I sent them out to find the gardener."

"Why?"

"Well, I mean . . ." She's appalled that I ask why. "Think of the damage he did."

"But think of the vegetables he grew."

"Rubbish. Anyone can grow vegetables. But he was dead."

"Really?" My heart or memory twists a little. Not very much, for after all, though an excellent gardener, he was an unwitting traitor.

"Yes. They found him in his hut. He'd been there for some time. People didn't call on him much, it seems."

"No. He was lonely."

"Well. It's a pity . . ." She looks dreamy again, cheated of her punishment for the gardener. "Are you going to stay here forever? Just sitting about?"

"I don't know."

"They won't take the slightest notice of you when I'm gone."

"Probably not."

She folds things in tissue paper, she has a special bag for shoes.

"We can't find the old woman. She's dead too, I expect."

"No! No!"

"I don't know what else she can be. She must be at least a hundred."

"She's not dead!"

"How do you know? Have you seen her?" Shrewd.

"No. I haven't seen her. I expect you're right. She must be dead." And buried under leaves, pine needles? Peaceful under leaves and pine trees? Hears the whip-poor-will complaining, hears the heron, the Shuh-shuh-gah, smiles at thoughts of Mudjekeewis, sings the song of Wah-wah-taysee to the little Hiawatha . . . ?

"Are you getting a bit simple?" she asks, friendly. "Perhaps it's something they did in the West Wing?"

"No," I say. "I've always been simple."

"That's true."

She whisks me to and from the office, she is organising things for the Board meeting, I can't keep up with her, I lag further and further behind.

"The other night," I say, pleading, "I came back here by myself. Do I have to go to the office with you any longer? Can't I just stay behind?"

"In a few days," she says kindly. "I do admit, you're quite useless."

"Won't you miss anyone?"

"Who, for God's sake?"

"Well . . . Hathaway?"

"Hathaway!" She laughs out of the corner of her face, the part she's not attending to at the moment. "You have to be joking!"

"But I thought . . . ?"

"He's impotent," she snaps. "He keeps his socks on."

"Oh . . ." I don't know what to say; as usual, I'm baffled. "I'm sorry."

"He likes to spank me with his ruler."

"Really?"

"Yes. It makes him feel big and powerful. God knows the ruler's bigger than he is." She giggles briefly. "Poor Hathaway."

"Well, then." For some reason I want to ask this. "What about . . . me?"

"*You?*"

"Will you miss me . . . at all?"

"Frankly"—she is being frank—"no. You're nothing but trouble."

"I suppose I do slow you down a bit."

"Well. You'll be happier on your own."

"Perhaps."

Though I can't imagine it. I did, after all, give birth to her in a way, she was part of me once. I know I am mooning about. There are so many things I want to know, but what are they?

"Will I . . . begin dreaming again?"

"I don't know. I shouldn't think so. I should think you're pretty well emptied out."

"It's true. I feel empty."

"You'll probably just . . . you know, wander off into the nineteenth century. Bake bread, bottle plums. That kind of thing."

"Cultivate my garden?"

She laughs. "I'd hate to see the garden."

"Yes. I'm not much good at gardening."

She hates to feel sorry for me. There's no need for her to feel sorry for me. Why does she do it?

"You could always learn," she suggests.

"Oh, no. I don't think so."

Later, I ask her, "Do I have to come to the Board meeting?"

"I don't know yet. We can probably manage without you."

"I hope so."

It is the day of the Board meeting. She is all packed, the suitcases closed and ready, waiting for a chauffeur to pick them up.

"I think you should put in an appearance," she says. "It would make things a lot easier."

"An appearance? What kind of appearance?"

"Just your usual. We're having a little . . . gathering before it starts. Just in case."

"In case . . . some of you aren't there when it's over?"

"Something like that."

"Hathaway for instance?"

She smiles, the mischief flaring. "Now, now. Don't jump to conclusions. You can leave before the meeting."

"You promise?"

She looks at me coldly, honestly. "I want you to leave before the meeting."

"All right." But I'm so reluctant.

"I shall be going then. The car is picking me up straight from the office. So I shan't see you again."

"All right. Good-bye."

She picks up her good handbag, takes a last look round.

"Jesus, I'll be glad to be out of this room. How can you stand it?"

"I hope you're . . . successful," I say awkwardly.

"I will be. And I hope"—she actually pats my cheek—"you'll be whatever you want."

"Peaceful."

"If that's your scene. Peaceful."

* * *

For the last time into the biting air, up in the elevator, past the plants in ceramic pots. We walk straight in now, no knocking. Hathaway is there, a misty glass in his hand. And the Director. I immediately look to his feet, finding handsome leather shoes, though I know he has black hairs on his toes. There is no mention of our previous meetings; in fact he says he is so pleased to meet her, he has heard so much about her, is so grateful and so on. A few members of the Committee are there. The gathering is a little muted, nervous. When someone laughs, it sounds like a dog barking in the night. I go up to the Director, tapping him on the arm.

"Where did they bury my dog?"

"The gardener, I'm sure . . ."

'The gardener is dead. Where did he bury her?"

"I'm terribly sorry. I haven't the faintest idea."

Suddenly, for the first time in the office, they see me. I stand in the middle of the room, bedraggled and haughty. Demanding the whereabouts of my dog's grave. She is appalled, she tugs at me, I refuse to budge.

"I'm not going," I say, "until you tell me where the dog is buried."

They consult hastily together. They must get rid of me. Time is running short, the Board meeting due to begin. The secretary runs into the outer office, runs back again, leafing through an old file.

"In the vegetable garden," she says. "By the green-house."

"Is there a sign?"

"Yes. Yes, I think so . . ." She is so flustered, both women so flustered.

"The sign says . . . it says Dead Dog."

"Thank you."

I walk to the door. Will they catch me now, hurry me away into some cell? They daren't. They are all silent, staring at my departure. She, my enemy, the assistant, takes a step forward, as though about to say something, but I silence her with a look, my look gags her.

My last sight of them is of a group of paralysed people, Hathaway's glass is halfway to his mouth. I know it is the last martini he will ever drink. The Director's face is all awry, nose twisted to one side, mouth gauping. The secretary looks arrested in flight. The others stand stiffly in ridiculous positions. Only she is still breathing.

"Good-bye," I say, going.

"Good-bye," she says, and raises her hand a little.

* * *

I know you will be there, on the stone bench. And there you are. I try to look at you closely, at last and for the one

194

and only time invited here. But I can't seem to recognise you, though of course I know who you are, and that you know me. You don't say anything, however, You just sit, basking in the morning sun; wondering how you got here, perhaps, though not where it will all lead.

I know well enough to walk backwards and to take myself with me, though I keep my eyes on you (wary, now) until you diminish, dwindle, become no more than a speck in the distance, between the two parallel lines that will never meet, or meet only in infinity. At last you are out of sight. That being done, I need never do it again. I can turn and face the mansion, walking lightly and eagerly, released from a prodigious weight.

21

This morning, after breakfast, I went to find where they had buried the dog. It was hard to remember the way to the vegetable garden, but I did it. The sight of the vegetable garden distressed me, everything overgrown, peas and beans flourishing among the weeds, marrow squash lying about anyhow, cabbages gone to seed, dead stumps of asparagus, potatoes rioting all over the place, it was appalling. When I reached the greenhouses I saw the glass broken, shrivelled tomato plants, even the frames rotting. I pushed through Aaron's rod, old man's beard and hemlock and found the board, quite neatly carved: Dead Dog. I didn't feel any grief, but was glad to know where the dog was buried.

"It's disgraceful," she said, "when you think of so many people starving. I suppose they buy everything frozen now. The waste."

"I'm so glad to see you. They told me you were dead."

"Oh, I will be. Someday."

"I hope not."

"It depends what you mean, doesn't it?" She looked up at me, her old face sharp and wicked. "I'm certainly not going to be cheated of dying, if that's what you mean. It must be the most interesting experience. However . . ."

She seemed to lose track of her thoughts for a few moments, prodding the dry earth with her rubber-tipped stick. "Compost," she said. "Good compost. That's what it needs."

"I came to see where they'd buried the dog."

"Ah, yes. She was a nice little dog. I remember her. She must have done the earth good, you know, when she rotted."

"Yes. I suppose so."

"Coffins deprive the earth. So long as they make quite sure there's no danger of disease they should do without coffins. Perhaps you would see to that when the time comes."

"If you insist."

"I do insist. I most certainly do." She went quite pink and would have stamped her foot if she hadn't needed both to stand on. I took her arm, almost crouching to reach it, and we began to creep slowly up the path.

"You mustn't think harshly of him, you know. He was an unhappy man. They'll have to plough it up if they leave it much longer, plough it all up and start again. What a waste. The trouble was, he was dreadfully intolerant. Well, there we are. What's past can't be mended. How are you getting along, dear?"

"I'm not sure yet."

"No. Well, of course. You can't be sure yet. Have you heard from the boy?"

"Which boy?"

"*I* don't know," she said rather wildly, waving her stick at a graveyard of brussel sprouts. "Any boy."

"No. I haven't."

"He'll come back in time. It breaks your heart, I know, but there it is, it's only a phase. If you give them an inch they take a mile. That's what comes of spoiling them."

"Did I spoil him . . . them?"

"Of course you did. Don't you remember the house?"

"Yes. I remember the house."

197

"I'm glad you're out of it. Of course, it was necessary. But I'm glad you're out of it. And what about your friends?"

"Which friends?"

"Adam . . . Hugh . . . Bill? George? Was his name George?"

"It might have been."

"Of course rotting vegetation has something to be said for it. Life to life, I think, would be far more suitable than ashes to ashes. If it comes to that, please see that they're put round the roses."

"Your ashes."

"Roses are gluttons for ashes. Where was I? What news of Basil Gondzik?"

"I don't know. He's still in the West Wing."

"Yes, I sometimes see him looking out of the window when I'm weeding. I'm surprised they don't put him onto this, a strong man like him, he might make a success of it, far more healthy than staying shut up in that room. I shall suggest it."

"You?"

"Why not? I shall write them a note. I'm very relieved that unpleasant person left you, you couldn't possibly have gone on living with her, sharing the same room. Good riddance, I thought, when I heard she'd gone."

"You know the story you told me?"

"Story? What story?"

"About Dora. Who grew up and had a great many babies and grew old and died."

"Oh, that story. Yes?"

"Was it true? Is that what really happened?"

She stopped, squinting up at me, leaning on my arm and on the stick. "There was a baby, you know. I was the first to see her."

"I know that." I was impatient. "But the story . . ."

"Ah. Well . . . perhaps . . ." She knew I was full of suspense, the old witch I belonged to. "Perhaps . . . I was wrong."

"Then what happened?"

She looked at me hard, her eyes boring into my skull. "Wait and see," she said, maddeningly.

"But . . ."

"What must be, must." She dug her stick into the path, moving forward. "If you can't have the crumb—"

"You must have the crust."

"Very good." She giggled, her small face crumpling horizontally. "It's a long lane?"

"That has no turning."

She shook with silent laughter. "It's always dark . . ."

". . . est before dawn. Every cloud has—"

"A silver lining," we chanted in unison.

"A stitch in—"

"Time saves nine."

"Too much haste—"

"Less speed. And you aren't the only pebble on the beach," she said with finality.

I walked with her to the edge of the woods, then she said she could manage. Believing her, I let go of her arm. She swayed a little, righted herself.

"Shall I see you again soon?" I asked.

"I'm sure you will."

"I don't know where you live . . . or anything."

"You know, I have a great admiration for Sir William Temple. Had, perhaps I should say. He said, 'Something like home that is not home is to be desired; it is found in the house of a friend.' Do remember that if you can."

"All right," I said.

"Run along now. You've got a long life tomorrow."

At least, I think that's what she said. That is what I heard. I turned away reluctantly, and when I looked back she was pottering through the trees, prodding the pine trees with the end of her stick and muttering something, no doubt about their upkeep.

* * *

It is very dark, even though it must be mid-day: all my lights are on, the dense trees sway and toss, toss and sway in distress or welcome. But the rain cannot manage it, cannot break out. My blinds clatter against the windows, birds could be heard screaming if it weren't for the roar of the dry storm.

The wind rushes off to the mountains to torment lakes and gorges I suppose. The air settles, heat comes back: no sun, but the air is sopped with rain that will not rain. Every cubic foot of air weighs a ton. People are dying. Because there is no sun, there is no shade. Even in the office they must be sprawling in their shirt-sleeves. The housekeepers (one less) blow down the front of their white overalls, drudging away with ancient carpet sweepers, the dust is so damp that it wets their dusters. Nobody goes outside. They examine atlases of old worlds, read the old books, prising the pages apart. They are drawn to the indoor fountain, which drips in its grotto watched over by bronze Prometheus (holding light bulbs), by Homer and by *Amor Caritas*. They loaf barefoot on the marble floor, drinking in the sound of the fountain. Nobody thinks to dabble their feet in the shallow water. They believe it to be a mirage.

And then the shadows reappear like old stains on the burned grass. The terrace steams gently. Rays, shafts of Doré sunlight break through the sodden cumulus and suddenly there it is again: high summer, the distant lily pond perfectly clear, the statue untouched, the trees leaning on their shadows, the woods showing clearings of light.

I go to the pool again now, but I'm the only one. I swim naked under the high sun, protected by the water. A baby mole swims a width valiantly. When I scoop it out it tries to bite with its little needle teeth, scurries away, no thanks. I float, feet moving lazily as fins, turn and open my eyes, looking down on to the remote green tiles, seeing no memory but a few twigs, leaves, blown there by the storm. I want to stand in the water all day, my head lolling like a dying dahlia, a stalk of cuckoo-spit being revived by children.

I am so simple. My daft simplicity eases my mind, flows through my arms to limp hands. I feel grateful.

*　*　*

One day, crossing the landing in search of a book (*Jude the Obscure, Italian Villas and Their Gardens, Victorian Working Women,* I haven't decided) I meet Dominic for (it seems) the first time. He suggests we sit down on the yellow plush sofa, under the bust of an 1860 Madonna with her head on one side. We are surrounded, of course, by lamps, some of them lit. I am uneasy again.

"How have you been?" Dominic asks, delicately lifting his dark glasses to rest the bridge of his nose.

"Very well. And you?"

"Well. Naturally, I'm delighted."

"What delights you?" Of course I can think of many things: the new weather, the books, the smell of floor polish, the mole in the pool.

"They've all been replaced. Haven't you heard? He's resigned. They've sent him to Agattu, Los Testigos, I'm not certain. He says he's going to take up some local craft or other."

"But that's wonderful!" I can hardly believe it and yet know that Dominic, being blind, wouldn't lie. "That's incredible! What happens now?"

"Well, naturally . . . I'm making a very careful selection."

"*You* are?"

"I was elected," he says modestly; then, with a good touch of spirit, "I've worked bloody hard, it wasn't easy. There's a lot to be done."

I want to kiss him, hug him, but have always been in slight awe of Dominic. He is a good man, and there's a degree of goodness beyond my comprehension. I have so many questions.

"What happened to Hathaway?"

"He took his wife's advice. It was unpleasant. We buried

him behind the garage, if you'd like to take a look sometime. I think there's a sign, or there should be."

"And his . . . assistant?"

"Oh . . . she'd left, of course. I hear she's doing very well in her own way."

"But if she came back . . . ?"

"We'd have to deal with her. Of course."

"What would you do?"

"I'm not sure. Some people, you know, are incorrigible."

"But would you use . . . violence?"

"I hope not. I very much hope not. I'm glad I came across you, by the way."

I'm pleased, the usual effect of flattery. "You could have found me before."

"No. I wanted to wait and see. I think I'm pretty certain now. Would you like to work for us?"

"Oh, no!" I'm quite horrified. "No! Certainly not!"

He smiles. "Very well. I know you support us, anyway."

"Yes. Of course I do. But I don't want to work for anybody. I've got too much to do."

"Really? That's good. What kind of thing?"

"Well, there's this place. I haven't started to explore it properly. Once I tried to make a map, but it was useless, I want to make another."

"Excellent. We shall need maps. If you want any help . . ."

"Thank you." I'm so excited, I really want to throw streamers and play in a brass band. Dominic is so calm. "What will you do here?"

"Reconstitute it. It'll take a long time. Get a few children in, probably."

I have a momentary, dreadful vision of the mansion becoming the house, chaos on every landing. "What for?"

"To be taught. It's useless having all these teachers here if there's no one to be taught."

"And the books."

"Of course. They need reading. Besides, children will . . . run about the place. Paddle in the fountain, maybe."

"Yes. They'll grow up, too."

He grins widely, most unsuitable for Dominic. "I sincerely hope so. That would be the whole point."

We sit silent for a moment, considering our different kinds of pleasure, our amazing future. "And Gondzik?"

"I was going to ask your advice about Gondzik. He's getting on very well. Rowena visits him every day now. You probably knew that?"

"No. But I'm very glad. Very glad."

"I thought you would be. Simon, by the way, sends his love."

"Sends . . . ?"

"He was very helpful after he left. I think he found it easier to commit himself, I mean from the outside. We've been in constant touch."

Constant touch. I make do with constant touch. "But he won't come back?"

"On, no. He's doing great things where he is. . . . Now about Gondzik."

"Yes."

"We've had various suggestions. What do *you* think?"

"I think he should be put in charge of the vegetable garden. It's a disgrace, the mess it's in. He's a strong man, he could make a success of it."

"Excellent!" Now Dominic is as excited as I was. "Excellent idea! I'll see to it immediately!"

"Perhaps he could live . . . with Rowena . . . in the gardener's hut? It's quite warm and dry. The gardener made it comfortable. Though they'll need a larger bed."

"Of course! Of course! I knew I could count on you!"

"But not to work."

"Oh, no." He actually gives me a kiss, all my brothers, my friends, my companions. "We won't put you to work. Just . . . well, keep going."

He dances off, Dominic exuberant, Dominic reconstituting life, blind and bold, in no danger of mistletoe.

I call after him:

"Dominic?"

"Yes?"

"Do you think I'm simple?"

"Of course!" he answers happily; the prisms tinkle, the fountain splashes downstairs, the stained-glass light twinkles on the tattered Aubusson.

* * *

This is my room, where I hope to live forever, which you will never see. The four doors are all open, so there is a through draught; the blinds flap back and forth in the draught. The door with the black cloth leads to a balcony, where I sometimes sit in the evenings; the one behind the screen leads, quite sensibly, out into the passage. My bathroom is still difficult, but I am growing plants on the shelves and someday hope to furnish it. Perhaps I shall put linoleum on the floor.

Mrs. April comes to see me occasionally. She is a new woman. She slaves for Dominic, though Dominic doesn't wish to be slaved for. She goes to see Gondzik's child, who plods about the orchard within a safe distance from the hut. Mrs. April takes her pine cones and butter nuts. Rowena, the child's mother, puts them on a high shelf when Mrs. April has gone. Gondzik works most of the time, stripped to the waist in the vegetable garden. We have fresh peas again and very small carrots, not to mention chicory and watercress.

I have accepted the fact that I'm simple and live through old songs. The children, as they grow up, don't seem to despise me for it. You have politely vacated my dreams, leaving me in order. I live at a long distance from everything I knew, seeing it very clearly. My maps are not only useful, they have a certain charm, cherubs blowing winds at every corner, boats on oceans, mountains and valleys very meticulous, though the scale is small. I think that after going to the pool today I will visit Gondzik's child and tell her a story.

September 1973